THE EFFECT OF FROST ON SOUTHERN VINES

ABOUT THE AUTHOR

Sandra Bunting grew up on the east coast of Canada and was awarded a BA in Radio and Television Arts from Ryerson in Toronto. After working for CBC News, Toronto, she moved to Europe and lived in France, Spain, and Ireland. She received Masters in Writing from National University of Ireland, Galway. Her first poetry collection, *Identified In Trees*, was published there by Marram Press. She returned to Canada in 2011 and established herself in Montreal and Northern New Brunswick.

Sandra is currently on the editorial board of the Galway based literary magazine, *Crannóg* and at the helm of her own independent publishing imprint, Gaelóg Press. She is a member of the Quebec Writers' Federation, Elan (The English Language Arts Network), the New Brunswick Writers' Federation, the Montreal Press Club and the Galway Writers' Workshop.

In 2012 she was awarded a Glenna Luschei award for poetry through the 'Prairie Schooner', University of Nebraska. She was runner-up for the 2006 Welsh Cinnamon Press First Novel Competition and was a finalist at the 2009 Irish Digital Media Awards for her Blog: Writing a Novel Online.

www.sandbunting.com

also by the author:

Identified in Trees (Poetry)

THE EFFECT OF FROST ON SOUTHERN VINES

stories

Sandra Bunting

Published by Gaelóg Press
409 Burnt Church Road
Burnt Church E9G 4C9
New Brunswick, Canada.
gaelogpress@gmail.com

www.sandbunting.com
sandra.bunting@gmail.com

ISBN: 978-0-9880992-0-3

The characters and events portrayed in this book are fictitious. Any similarity to real persons, living or dead, is coincidental and not intended by the author.

Thanks to the editors of Crannóg, BíPí and Criterion where some of these stories were first published.

Book and Cover Design: www.Cyberscribe.ie
Cover image: Wolfgang Zwanzger www.20er.net

TABLE OF CONTENTS

THE CORNER HOUSE

Michael and Paul climbed over the wall of the orchard, the pockets of their short trousers bursting with apples, their daily route during the summer holidays almost at an end. They met each morning at the top of the street and crossed the big road that led them out of the familiar rows of city-centre terraced houses, and over to the canal where they threw rocks at pigeons and floated pieces of wood to race. Dogs followed them, the usual entourage of a collie, a Labrador, a mixed greyhound-wolfhound and a weird little terrier. Michael's cat sometimes followed as well but it usually slinked off into the bushes by itself somewhere along the way to chase birds or other small animals.

"We were lucky there, Paul," said Michael, the smaller of the two, struggling to catch his breath. "I think yer man was waiting for us. He's cottoned on to when we're going to show up. We have to change our schedule."

He sat down on the pavement.

"Perhaps we should give it a rest for awhile. They say old Fletcher's a mean bastard. I wouldn't like to be at his mercy."

"Sure, we're not going to get caught. We just have to be smarter. It wouldn't be any fun if he just invited us into the

7

orchard. 'Help yourself to as many apples as you like lads'," he mimicked. "What fun is there in that?"

"They say there's a holy well in there and if you drink from it, good things happen to you."

"What would you want with something like that? Don't we have to make our own way in the world, same as anyone else?"

"I only thought…with my ma being sick…."

"Sure she's going to be fine."

Strains of 'The West's Awake' rose up and they knew the postman would soon be rounding the corner on his bike. The retinue of dogs, who had earlier deserted the boys for a more interesting expedition, followed at his heels, barking a little out of tune.

"How are ya, lads? Fine day today."

The postman said the same thing everyday. It could be lashing rain, a gale force wind or hailstones falling all around. The postman always had a smile.

> *… that Connacht lies in slumber deep.*
> *But, hark! a voice like thunder spake,*
> *The West's awake! The West's awake!*

Paul and Michael followed him to the end of the street where a group of men and older boys were leaning against the corner house talking.

"How are ya lads?" called the postman, to which the men nodded.

The two boys went around to the back of the houses and searched in the long grass for a ball they had left behind. They gave it a few kicks, ran back to where the men were standing and practiced against the wall of the opposite house until the older boys joined in and they had the makings of a match. Cars always gave priority to games on the street.

"How's yer ma?" asked one of the big boys.

Michael shrugged. He knew he didn't need to answer. Nothing could happen on the street that wasn't common knowledge.

The men disappeared from the pavement all of a sudden. The older boys, too, tried to make a getaway but were too slow. A large man with white hair appeared in front of them and consulted a notebook.

"I can't believe there is no-one at home in any of these houses. Don't they have work to do, children to mind?"

One of the older boys winked at Michael and Paul and they took off through the lane to warn the other houses.

"The bishop's man is here to collect for the new church again," they whispered.

Neighbours, sitting out to catch a few rays of sunshine before turning to their chores again, gathered up their chairs. Those stopping to share news hurried on their way. No one ventured out until they were certain the danger had passed.

"I'd rather give any extra I had to the Caseys, who are having a hard time of it, with Mary so sick," commented an elderly woman, who had a small shop in the front room of her house.

Michael's father had wanted him to go out to the country to stay with his elderly grandfather and help on the farm. His friend Paul's mother, however, offered to keep him with them.

"Well as long as you don't keep running home and bothering your mother," his father warned.

The next morning Michael was reluctant to climb over the wall into the orchard.

"The old man will surely be waiting for us," he said.

"But we have to. We have to get water from the holy well to make your mother better."

Paul didn't tell Michael that he had filled a small jar with water from the tap at home, closed the top on tight and put it in the pocket of his short trousers. Just in case they didn't get it at the old man's.

While Michael held back, Paul hoisted himself up on the wall and jumped into the forbidden orchard.

"I caught you this time you little f----er. You'll pay your way now for all you've pilfered."

Michael waited near the wall for ages. When his friend failed to turn up, he wandered down to the corner to stand with the men.

"Where's your little friend?" they asked.

"Caught by old man Fletcher in the orchard."

The men shook their heads.

"Not good," they said. "He's a right bastard."

Michael gave a little shudder.

Just before dinner time, Paul came walking down the street. Michael ran up to him.

"I thought you were a goner," he said.

"He's not so bad. He just put me to work, is all. Look. He gave me this." He held out a basket of apples.

"Apple tart tomorrow, or what?"

And then he slapped his head as if he had just remembered something.

"And I got some water out of that holy well you were talking about."

Michael didn't know if it was the water that made his mother better but she improved rapidly not long after drinking it. Paul just winked. Soon Michael was able to move back to his own home.

* * *

Strong afternoon sun hit the wall of the corner house, which also served as protection against the wind. Michael, half dozing, adjusted his hat and looked up towards the old orchard, now a distillery. A few of the other men joined him as they finished their shifts. Younger lads played on the streets with their skateboards or kicked a soccer ball.

"What do you think of the new ones?" Michael asked, patting the wall.

"Ah sure they're nice enough," said the man next to him.

"The kids are driving them demented though. Breaking their flowerpots. Knocking on their windows. Throwing their ball into the back garden."

After going home for their dinner, the men gathered again that night. In the middle of a smoke and chat, they heard a door fling open and heavy footsteps coming towards them.

"I told you kids before ..." shouted a neatly dressed man in his early thirties.

The group of heavy-set middle-aged men looked up at him in astonishment.

"I'm sorry. I thought it was kids. We've been having trouble."

The men didn't say a word. They just threw their cigarettes down on the pavement, pulled down their caps and ambled off.

* * *

For years no one leaned against the wall of the corner house. The men didn't do it out of respect for the new owners, James and Michelle Horan. The teenagers who had tormented them had grown up. Neighbours would nod to the couple on the street and they grew to like and depend on their presence. James organised committees to go to city hall to stop the encroachment of business threatening the residential nature of the community. There was always something to fight.

Not everything he did, however, appealed to the neighbours! He raised money and put a bench in the small green area at the end of one terrace. A bunch of winos claimed it immediately and kept people up in the nearby houses for nights. The bench had to be removed.

James applied for a grant for a Heritage Study of the area so its 'unique' history would be preserved. It was launched at the local pub with many invited dignitaries.

"Thousands of euro for this?" one of the men remarked. "Sure all he had to do was ask old Tommy Brandan."

"I wouldn't pass up a pint of Guinness and a few sandwiches."

"But aren't we paying for them, having to listen to them speeches?"

"Ah sure, we can just lose ourselves in the corner."

Then there was the huge meeting about the site at the top of the road. The whiskey distillery had become a woollen mill employing many of the local men and women. However, with time, the mill finally closed its doors and moved to the outskirts of the city. There were several proposals for the old site. One was for apartment units, another for a hotel and one for a shopping centre.

James Horan started the discussion. "We have the right to say what we want in our community."

"If only he knew what it was like before," Michael whispered. "Rows and rows of apple trees. Blossoms in spring. Fruit in summer. The holy well."

At the end of the meeting James announced that he would be away for a year doing consultancy work in Africa.

"I'll hand everything over to you," he said. "I'm going to rent out my house. But I'll be back. This is my home."

Michael watched as cleaners and decorators came to do up the Horan house. Some of the local lads helped Michelle put boxes up in the attic and another with a tall ladder cut the ivy, cleaned out the gutters and gave the windows a scrub. Many in the street came to wave goodbye to James and Michelle as they drove away in a luggage-packed taxi to the airport on the first leg of their journey to Africa.

* * *

The factory was torn down to make way for a hotel. Some of the neighbours were happy.

"They're putting in a leisure centre. We can go for a swim, have a massage."

"And do you think it won't cost you?"

Others were bitter that they no longer had jobs. They were hoping the hotel would take them on.

A cigarette was passed around. Out of the breeze, the warm sun streamed once again onto the men who lined the wall of the corner house. Michael looked up to the top of the road. When he squinted, by trick of the sun, he could almost see the apple trees, the way things used to be. He felt an itch on his back and rubbed it against the rough stone of the wall. "Nice of the Horans to clear the ivy," he thought.

A bicycle that had been racing down the street suddenly screeched to a halt.

"How are you lads?" the driver nodded. "Still daydreaming, Michael?"

"By the Jaysus, I was just thinking of the time you got caught by old man Fletcher. How long are you home for?"

"Ach, the marriage broke up in Australia. Thought I'd come home for a while. Spend some time with the old ones."

Paul lay the bike down on the curb and leaned his back against the wall with the rest of the men.

"God, that feels good. Twenty years since I've done that, lads," he sighed. He took a few notes from his pocket. "This is great. Standing here and doing nothing! How much is the membership, lads? I'm back."

"We're all back," said Michael. "Back on the corner."

HEART-SHAPED

The family was going on a camping trip to France. Julia Ryan had never been that far away from Ireland before. Looking out the plane window, there were white fluffy clouds underneath her. That's why she wasn't scared. If the plane fell, or if she was somehow outside the plane, she would land on a bed of soft fleece. Up here, the sky was blue and the sun was shining. On the ground it had been raining.

Later there was a tickle in her tummy as they hit land with a bump. It was still sunny down on the ground, so it had to be France. She followed her parents and her older sister Annie through customs feeling very proud and grown up with her own passport. She listened as her parents tried out their French to pick up the rented car they had reserved. It was tiny but it was red and shiny. It looked a bit like a ladybird without the spots.

They managed to get the luggage, the tents and sleeping bags in the boot so they weren't cramped in the back seat. It was a long drive to the campsite and it was hot. Green fields gave way to tightly packed sunflowers and corn, tall and proud against the wispy blue sky. The earth was pale and dusty and looked as if it might crumble. There was a mixed scent of rose and lavender.

The campsite was outside the village in a little wood with a stream running through it. Mr. Ryan got out the tents. They were brand new. Julia and Annie had a bright yellow one to themselves while their parents had a slightly bigger one in navy blue.

By the time they got things set up, it was time for dinner. There was a communal barbecue and picnic site on the other side of a clump of trees but the Ryans had no food. The village was just a short drive away. But when they got there, shutters were closed on most of the houses and although it was still light, there were no people on the street. Perhaps it was a ghost town.

At the bottom of the street, they saw a light shining from a pizza restaurant. They were brought to a tiny courtyard that looked liked someone's back yard, containing three patio tables with umbrellas sticking out of them. There were trees growing out of the pavement and potted flowers all around. An attractive woman at the next table was finishing her dessert. She had a white poodle in her lap and she let it jump up and lick her face. She returned the kisses and made cooing noises to the dog to the disgust of Mr. Ryan.

They just made it back to the campsite before the gates closed at ten o'clock. The ground was lumpy and a fly had got in the tent. Annie annoyingly went on and on about the boys in her class and sang all the songs she learned in her performance school. Then there were strange noises like something jumping on the tent.

Julia's ten-year-old self had wanted to crawl in with her parents but she was too frightened to open the flap. She was also happy to be independent and didn't want to let on that she was scared. Light seeped through the thin material of the tent and when she unzipped it, she saw long-eared rabbits hopping around the site.

Julia's parents, tired after the long drive, were still sleeping. Annie had just woken up. They both dressed quickly and went out to explore the grounds. There was a central building with toilets, showers and washing machines. There were picnic tables, a little patio to have dinner, a playground off to the side. That seemed to be it – no shop, no pool, no café.

When Julia's parents got up, they drove into the town to get supplies. Everything was different at the supermarkets but the girls were able to pick out what they wanted by the pictures on the packaging. They then visited a castle with knight's armour, secret passages and a wardrobe with hidden drawers for jewels, love letters or poison. Julia could imagine an alchemist making potions in the high towers and prisoners suffering horrors in the dungeon that was filled with bows, lances, swords and those balls with spikes. Although she felt at home within the thick walls, it was good to get out among colourful hollyhocks and cool oak trees.

For lunch they bought two long baguettes with cheese and ham and shared them. That night they brought food to cook at the barbecue. Annie was helping her mother while Julia just sat at the picnic table watching some children play. She was daydreaming when a ball landed at her feet.

Behind the ball was a boy who looked about ten, her age. Soft light brown curls fell around his tanned face.

Julia kicked the ball back to him. A few minutes later the ball landed at her feet again. She looked up and saw the boy looking at her, and she kicked it back to him again.

"Do you want to play?" he asked in a very English accent.

Julia nodded and walked over to the others waiting for the ball. They were all French. The boy spoke to them in French and to Julia in English.

"Julia, dinner," her mother called.

Julia started to walk away. She had never had good social skills. Perhaps it was shyness. Sometimes she didn't know what to do in certain situations, so she did nothing. The boy ran up to her.

"Will you play tomorrow?" he asked.

"Maybe," said Julia.

The next day the females in the family went shopping. Perfume shops offered hours of enjoyment. The different shapes and colours of the bottles were exquisite. There was even cologne for cats. Free samples came with each purchase. It was great to be pampered. They went on to roam through the clothes shops. Julia convinced her mother that she needed a new green T-shirt and matching trousers for school.

The boy came over, kicking the ball, as soon as Julia sat down at the picnic tables.

"I'm Peter," he said.

"I'm Julia."

"I know," said the boy.

They played a bit of football but Julia found that she couldn't run in her new trousers. Peter said he had had enough too and they both walked back to the picnic table where Peter's father was drinking wine with her parents.

"Peter's mother is English. That's why he speaks so well," her mother explained.

Julia looked impassive. "When is dinner?" she asked.

"It will be a little while yet," said her mother.

Julia looked at Peter who took her by the hand and dragged her off.

"There's something I have to show you."

He brought her to a tree fort built in a huge oak. They climbed high into the branches and laughed at anyone who walked under it. They jumped on tire swings on another tree. He showed her the little stream where they caught a frog. Then Peter told her to follow him to a very special place. She found herself walking down an incline into a natural cave. It was like going into a large room. Light poured in from the opening.

Peter put his hand on the wall of the cave and scooped out the porous earth.

"There used to be a tunnel from here down to that big chateau. But it caved in."

Julia poked a finger in the wall. Maybe the hole she made would be there forever.

"You could almost live here."

"There are thousands of caves around here. Some people do live in them."

Julia's imagination ran away with her.

"Imagine scooping out your own home," she said.

A shadow passed over the mouth of the cave. A dog perhaps but it reminded them that it was late.

"We had better get back. We can come again tomorrow."

When the family wasn't off touring, Julia was with Peter. They played football, went on the swing and explored the caves. However, the night before they were to leave Julia looked for Peter but he wasn't around.

The family, having organized everything for the journey the following day, were seated in front of their tents looking at the stars for the last time from that particular place. Peter appeared. He went over to Julia and handed her something. It was a large rock of the same kind of material found in the caves. It was naturally shaped like a heart but Peter had drawn another smaller one in pink crayon in between their two names. She looked at it and smiled but when she raised her head and saw everybody staring at her in expectation, she threw it to the ground, ran into the tent and cried herself to sleep.

Peter was there the next morning but not only did Julia refuse to say goodbye, she kept her head down and would not look at him. Annie felt sorry for him, picked up the rock, put it in the boot and said good-bye.

The new campsite on the Seine was more elaborate. There was a swimming pool, water slide, tennis courts, crazy golf and a playground. The actual sites were not as nice though. There weren't as many trees. It was more open and not as private. Mr. Ryan got out the two tents and started to assemble them but the ground was hard and the pegs wouldn't go in. He looked around for something to bang them with. Julia was sent off to look for a rock but she came back empty-handed. It didn't matter anyway because her father had managed.

"How were you able to get them in the ground?" Julia asked.

Her father shrugged.

"I found this old rock in the boot of the car. It was a bit soft but it did the job. Good thing we had it."

Julia looked towards the bushes he was pointing to. Lying there was the stone. It was broken in two, right through the middle of the painted heart. One half said "Peter." The other half said "Julia." Her father hadn't noticed because he never noticed those kinds of things.

She threw one half of the rock deeper into the bushes and picked up the one that said "Julia" and placed it in the boot again, smiling for the first time since they left the old campsite.

On the plane back home, Julia looked down on the clouds as she had done on the journey there. Although still fluffy, they appeared almost flimsy and not as much of a safety blanket as they had before. The holiday photos had been developed before they left France. Julia took out the one of Peter and hid it in her pocket, looking at it from time to time, not because she was in love but because it made her feel good.

DRESSED AS A GODDESS

The grant application for an assistant looked good. If all went well, he could have another person working with him before Easter. However, for the moment, it looked as if he would have to lock up the place as usual for a month and leave it to Mrs. O'Hehir to look after. A month off to do research was part of the agreement when he took up the job. January was a quiet month. It was good to get away from the endless rain and fierce winds of the west of Ireland. Every time he came back, his friends would rhyme off a litany of illnesses they had suffered and overcome.

Home! Home for Dr. Geoffry Mulvihill was his place of work. The purpose-built, modern building in the centre of town came with the job. He remembered his footsteps sounding through the empty rooms as he walked through the new museum for the first time. There were only two instructions: fill it and look after it. He had lived up to his part of the bargain. All his creativity, contacts and powers of persuasion had been used in fundraising. There was not one grant application that he did not look at and try to find out how it could relate to the museum. Filling the building was not a problem. There was a hodgepodge of items left over from the old museum. People had been generous about donating what they thought was important to their heritage. Whatever opinion he had on these items, he respected the wishes of the residents and devoted a room in their honour. Other artefacts were sent down from Dublin and the local council put some things aside after a decree from Europe to conserve all important local artefacts and monuments. Other rooms contained purchases made when there was money available.

His one indulgence – going back to his days as a lecturer in Egyptology – was a small room, a cubicle really, where he displayed a few statues of Egyptian Goddesses: Nut, Blast, Isis. Although more aesthetic than valuable, they were not without worth. Contacts made during his research month had paid off and allowed him to purchase minor treasures on the museum's delicate budget. He printed up a leaflet with details on each of the statues together with some general information. The room had proved popular but perhaps not in the way the museum curator could have imagined.

Not long after he established it, women started coming to visit the "goddess room" to meditate. Dr. Mulvihill found out that a local woman had started a "goddess workshop." Her brochure stated "Find the Goddess Within. Ten Week course on how to improve your life by finding the power." Geoffry tried to counter the so-called nonsense by writing scholarly articles, which he printed and distributed. He also gave interviews to the press. These measures, however, did not deter what he called the "goddess groupies" from their enthusiasm over his special room.

The board was pleased with his progress on fund-raising and acquisitions. Looking after them, however, was another matter. Each item had to be categorised, valued, restored (if applicable) and displayed. A fortune was spent on a security system and insurance premiums went up with each new purchase.

The building and the items needed regular cleaning, something he had overlooked when he told the board he could handle everything himself. He just let the dust pile until he realised he was entitled to hire someone to clean. Mrs. O'Hehir kept the museum spotless ever since. An older lady, she knew how to dust without breaking artefacts and how to keep out of Dr. Mulvihill's hair while he was working. It was almost as much a home to her as it was to the curator. She would often be seen scrubbing floors late into the night, no question of overtime. She would go about her work with pride and a sense of responsibility.

There was one room however she would not go into. "Those hussies!" she said. To his amusement, Dr. Mulvihill discovered she was talking about the Egyptian statues. So he took care of the little goddesses himself. One day, thinking about the ending of a paper he had to present that week, he looked in on the room to give it a quick dust. There in front of the statue of Nut was a woman with long caramel-coloured hair stretching her arms above her head. She was completely naked.

"Where are your clothes?" asked Dr. Mulvihill, trying to look down at the floor.

The woman ignored him.

"Listen," said Dr. Mulvihill. "This kind of thing is just not acceptable. I suppose that crazy woman told you to look for the goddess within. Well, you won't find anything here."

The woman lowered her arms gently, sighed and looked at the curator.

"I am the crazy one who tells women to look for the goddess within."

She put out her hand for Geoffry to shake. "June Constance."

He shook her hand, averting his eyes from her pale shapely body.

"I'll be in my office" was all that he could manage.

Later June, now clothed, sat down in the chair opposite his desk as he told her the significance of each goddess statue. He was surprised at how much she knew and, although he still felt her views were a load of nonsense, he had a new respect for her.

He left the next day for Egypt. There was mention of a goddess on a newly found stone tablet that could form the basis of a new paper. Perhaps he'd also bring back a stature or some other item of antiquity. Leaving everything in the capable hands of Mrs. O'Hehir, he packed his laptop. There was no need for clothes. Some of his clothes were stored in Cairo with his guide. Anything else he could buy there cheaply.

At the airport in Dublin, a call came from the Council telling him that the funds had been approved to hire a new assistant. There was a catch though. To receive final approval, they needed to supply the name of the likely candidate. As

Dr. Mulvihill didn't want to put off his trip, he left it up to the board to hold interviews and hire someone, outlining the kind of person he was looking for and what he needed them to do.

* * *

The trip to Egypt was fruitful. Not only did Dr. Mulvihill get enough research material for another paper, he was bringing back a tablet covered with ancient hieroglyphics and engraved with the picture of an Egyptian goddess he had yet to identify. Besides that, he'd got warmth in his bones, colour in his face and felt relaxed and refreshed. He was ready to start back at the museum.

He arrived back on February 1st, the beginning of the Irish spring. The daffodils would soon be coming up even though the weather wasn't noticeably milder. It was the Feile Bríd, the feast of Bridget, herself a goddess, patron of poets. Mrs. O'Hehir had things opened up; everything was clean, the heat on, and coffee made.

"Welcome home," she said. Then corrected herself, "I mean, welcome back."

"Glad to be back," he looked at her tenderly," ... and home."

She smiled. Dr. Mulvihill took a parcel wrapped in newsprint out of his briefcase and gave it to the woman.

"Oh, Doctor. You shouldn't have."

Under the packaging was a silver teapot very much like an Aladdin's lamp. Unconsciously, she rubbed the side. No genie.

"It's for mint tea," said the boss.

"Thank you so much. You shouldn't have. And I'm sure it will do just as nicely with the 'Barry's'."

Formalities over, Dr. Mulvihill was anxious to get on with his work. He opened his laptop on his desk and transferred files to his desk computer. A pile of correspondence in his in-box begged for attention but that could wait. He unzipped a pocket of his laptop bag and took out another package wrapped in newspaper. He tore off the paper, brushed his hand across the tablet and became lost in its mysteries.

The tablet would need a special stand and perhaps a glass enclosure to protect it against deterioration. That was something to organise right away. Dr. Mulvihill walked towards the goddess cubicle. The fact was that he had missed the statues: the mystery of Nut, the playfulness of Blast, the beauty of Isis. However, entering the room, he almost dropped the new stone tablet. Instead of the sleek forms he expected to see, each of the statues was dressed in its own knitted costume: booties, dresses, matching hats. Isis even had a miniature handbag.

"Mrs. O'Hehir!" he called. But she didn't answer. It was a big place. She could be anywhere. Dr. Mulvihill left the statues as they were for the moment. He put the tablet on the floor while he took measurements for a glass case in the room. Perhaps all the statues should have better protection. He was back in his office, working on designs and measurements when a knock came on his door.

"Ah Mrs. O'Hehir, do come in."

The door opened. "You!" he said.

A hand went out to him.

"June Constance, your new assistant."

Dr. Mulvihill couldn't speak.

"I'll ring the board," he managed after a while. "There must be some mistake. I left instructions on what I wanted."

"Exactly. Major in Archaeology. Postgraduate in Heritage Studies."

"But …"

"They thought I'd complement you. I know more about the Celtic stuff." She smiled. "I know a little about your area too. Egyptology is fascinating."

"And all that nonsense about 'the goddess within'?"

"That too! Part of me."

Taking his glasses off to rub his eyes, Dr. Mulvihill sighed.

"Do you think you could at least keep your clothes on?"

The woman laughed.

"I hope I will still be able to visit the 'goddess room'," she said.

The curator remembered his last visit to the room and burst into gales of laughter.

"What's so funny? Can I go in there or not?"

To her puzzled look, he started laughing again. "Only when clothed," said Dr. Mulvihill, picturing the statues and their knitted outfits and then imagining his new assistant in similar attire. Perhaps she could get a matching orange and lime green knitted handbag similar to what Isis was now sporting.

"Mrs. O'Hehir will sort you out," he laughed. "You'll see. We'll all get on just fine.

THE EFFECT OF FROST ON SOUTHERN VINES

Lily sat brooding in the living room trying to ignore the existence of the photos that lay scattered on the kitchen table.

After pouring herself a glass of red wine, she went out onto the veranda, feeling the heat. In no time her simple pale pink silk dress clung to her body and she had to wipe her brow.

The enormous oak trees growing randomly in the front yard gave a sense of permanence. Spanish moss hung from their branches. "Prehistoric" her father had said. Lily had been frightened of it when she was a little girl. She imagined it would catch her in its net-like embrace, and pull her far up in the trees to digest her at its leisure. Her fifth birthday was ruined when she ran into a thick bit hanging loose and she thought it had tangled in her waist-long hair. She only calmed down after her mother carefully brushed her hair the hundred times she usually did before bedtime and assured her there was nothing caught in it.

Trees towered over the house Lily's great grandfather had built and that she now lived in with her boyfriend. She sat on the veranda swing of grey weathered wood. The colours of the house, the swing and the land pleased her. They were a mix between a grey and a green, an old colour, like the walls of an abandoned house. She flexed her feet as she swung and then, placing them on the floor, she tapped out the rhythm to a dance piece she had been trying to learn.

The tune was almost embedded in her mind when she saw her boyfriend's car. Its red stood out strongly against the washed out colours of the landscape. Max whistled as he approached her, knocking her dance tune out of her head. She couldn't berate him for that. He was pure music. That's just what he was.

"You look relaxed." Max smiled as he sat down beside her on the veranda.

Max knew not to mention the photos at that moment. He sat with her for a while, rocking back and forth. Then he kissed her lightly, a brush at the side of her head just under her hairline.

"I'll go and make dinner," he said. "I picked up some crayfish from Little Joe Boudreau. Shouldn't be too long."

Long before Max moved in with Lily he knew that he would be doing the cooking. At first he thought that Lily was watching her figure as a dancer as she helped herself to fruit and raw vegetables from the kitchen and offered them suggestively to him. Then he watched her wolf down dinners when they went out to a restaurant or when he had cooked a meal in his small apartment over JuJu's jazz club in town.

The sensuality of raw vegetables soon wore off when he moved in with her.

"Why don't you ever cook?" he asked.

"I don't know how. I guess Tilda always did it."

"And who is Tilda?"

"Our old maid."

And so Max took over the cooking and got a girl down the road to come in once a week to do the cleaning and the washing.

When the dinner was ready, Max went out on the veranda to call Lily. She was dancing, concentrating hard on some tune in her head. So he waited until she finished.

"That looks demanding."

"Yeah, it's a new piece by Jeff Brom. It's all solo work."

"That's great."

Afterwards Max got out his alto sax and played a couple of tunes that he would perform at the club later that night. He could see his music enter Lily, creep up through her and stroke her from inside. She closed her eyes and trance-like, swayed almost imperceptibly back and forth. Max gently put down the saxophone and with lips that had blown out those long melancholic notes, he kissed Lily, who responded in little waves. As she melted into him, he put his hands on her breasts and felt them come alive beneath the thin silk. He traced the outline of her lithe dancer's body and the smooth strength of her legs. Slower and gentler he let his fingers crawl up the inside of her leg until he cupped the essence of her, feeling her tingle and palpitate against his hand. When his fingers struck moisture, he felt himself straining at his trousers and moved to undo the zip.

Lily stirred. Now out of her trance, she straightened her body. "Not tonight, hon. I'm wrecked from dancing. I'm going to bed."

"Ah, Lily. Don't go yet. I have a half hour before I have to go to the club," Max said, getting up. "Ok then. I'll be right back."

In the toilet off the kitchen he wondered what was happening to them. It had been a month now. Lily didn't seem to have changed. She still responded to him. But always at the last moment ...

On the way back to the living room, he picked up the photos he had put away earlier. Lily cringed.

"I don't want to see them. I don't want to go."

"But Lily. You have never been out of the state. It will be good for you. For both of us"

"No, no, no," she said. "Things are just fine here the way they are. If you go, I'll wait for you."

She was flashing her eyes and giving her southern pout that he found so attractive.

"You know I have to go Lily. The music's not the same since Katrina. Most of the guys have stayed up north. I have to work with them on this. This composition has been in the works for years. It's going to blow the jazz world away. Six months is all it is, Lily. C'mon."

"But my dancing?"

"There are dance troupes up north. They're good. Maybe you could learn something new. Or you could learn to skate. Try out different muscles."

"Skate? Oh God, I forgot about the cold."

He got up from the sofa and put his saxophone in its case. He picked up his old black hat off the floor lamp, placed it on his head and opened the screen door.

"Just remember Lily. I am going up north to work on that composition. You can come with me or not. But I'm not going to stay lonely. Think about it."

* * *

Lily knew that it was not easy keeping an audience attentive during an hour and a half solo dance performance let alone having the stamina to be able to go on stage every night for a week. However, the music was powerful, allowing Lily, after so many weeks of strenuous practice, to move with abandonment. Although there was a lot of variety in mood, there was a theme to the piece. With interesting props such as old chests, old clocks and big old keys, there was a mixture of energetic and slow sensual bits. The reviews were enthusiastic.

Max took a night off from the club to attend. Lily could see him in the front row and when the slow undulating sections of the piece came, she danced for him. She remembered how she had danced for him when they first met. She'd reacted to the long breathy strokes of his saxophone, lazily twisting her body, the notes fingering her skin until she fell onto Max and, still feeling the instrument in her head, moved together with him until sunrise. Now, when she danced the slow part of the performance, she danced it as if she were with Max.

Before shows Lily would indulge in her hobby of searching on e-bay for vintage southern documents. She had just acquired a 1954 letter from the Mayor of New Orleans. 1954 was the year of her mother's birth. She'd previously paid five dollars for ten legal documents from the late 1800s.

She didn't know what she was going to do with all these papers but she liked having them. Each one seemed to tell a story and Lily would let her imagination free to fill in the rest. She could picture the clothes of the time, the vehicles, the music.

'The South' and her family's past had a strong pull on her. She was the last of a long line. However, despite all that, she knew she was going to say yes to Max. She had watched how women looked at him. They stared at his high leather boots and climbed up his tight black jeans and T-shirt to the old hat. They liked the way he moved and how he drew everything he could out of his saxophone, leaving it shining and breathless. Women wanted to be the saxophone in Max's arms. She would plan what she would pack for their journey north.

* * *

Lily tentatively put it in her mouth teasing the tip in little motions with her tongue. Then she moved up the stalk with long licks, closing her eyes with pleasure, progressing to an unbearable desire to put it deeper in her mouth and suck. Not used to the bulk, her throat closed involuntarily until what she had in her mouth dissolved to liquid and left her tingling.

She had been coming to the small outdoor skating rink in the middle of the park ever since it was cold enough to be made. As a southern girl, Lily had been frightened of the cold. And she froze. But in time she found that the exercise of skating gave her energy and warmed her up. At first she was wobbly on skates. She hadn't the control that she had with her feet on the ground in dancing. It was as if the mountain of trees and snow were inspiring her, coaxing her, teaching her. Starting with slow movements, she finally grew more confident and became graceful and powerful. The winter clothes were restrictive but not unbearably so.

One last turn quickly round and then home. There was usually no one else on the ice at that time. That is until recently! She had been noticing a tall man out of the corner of her eye. And today! Oh my! She had to rush home to Max. Composing or not composing, she needed him.

Skates over her shoulder, Lily flew through the park, crossed the street and ran up the three floors to their apartment.

"You're early, Sweet Bun. I'm not finished yet. We are trying it out tonight with the orchestra. I have to make changes."

Lily stood in the middle of the living room where Max worked. She flung her skates on the sofa. Not taking her eyes of Max, her mouth hungry, she started to undress slowly. First hat, mitten and scarf. Then her knee-high black leather boots. The fur-lined hooded ski jacket opened with a zip. Now all the sensuous motion of her dancing could be seen. She lifted her sweater over her head, distractedly brushing her breasts. Bending down, she removed her socks and turned around to move her bottom suggestively while her hands went to un-zip her jeans. As if it had been a dance, and in a way it was, she eased her T-shirt off and stood looking at Max in her bra and panties.

Max, who was stunned, jumped up from his composition and pulled her to him searching her mouth.

"Um, cold," he said.

"Icicle!" mumbled Lily.

As their tongues touched, warming their mouths, allowing them feel each other's softness, Max undressed and reached to undo Lily's bra strap. As he lowered the panties, he hoped she would not go cold on him at the last moment, as she had been doing for too long.

Max knew her body by touch. Eyes closed and still kissing her, he reached down to feel that she was moist. A soft moan told him to go on. He had never felt so hard. He guided them both to their knees and to the carpet. He took himself in his hand and pushed inside Lily. He felt like the dancer then. He was directed by movement. His head was exploding. To be inside Lily again! To be inside Lily! To ... be ... in ... side ...!

* * *

Lily had just finished a pirouette on ice. She had lost her fear of falling. Near the end of each practice she always saw the tall man out of the corner of her eye and always performed the same ritual on him with her mouth. One day, when the ice was starting to melt and she knew she wouldn't be able to skate outside anymore, she asked him his name.

"Frost," he said. "The name is Jack Frost."

IN CARIBBEAN BLUE

Victoria was struggling with a rumba. All the others were swinging their hips and flirting with the dancing instructors, their clothes hardly covering their tanned bodies. Looking down at her pale legs, Victoria stiffly tried to keep up with the rhythm but the rumba eluded her. She felt like a deranged elephant. The cleaning woman watching from the door, squeezed in next to her, stuck out her bottom and shook it, her arms moving as if she were a chicken. "I don't want to look like that," thought Victoria. But then the woman grabbed Victoria's arms and put them on her hips so she could feel the swaying movement. The women moved too fast.

Time to take a break. Besides, she had blisters on her feet and wasn't able to get plasters at the pharmacy. Shortages! The hot sun on her head was making her dizzy. There was no covering on the roof of the old pastel-blue colonial building. No barrier if she fell off. From the next roof, she could hear pigs and chickens.

Skipping the afternoon dance class, she thought vaguely of buying last minute souvenirs. But in the end, she just strolled along the *Malecon*. It reminded her a bit of the Promenade at home where she walked every day, the spray soaring up over the breakwater of boulders. The colours were different however. Grays and silvers at home. Here the blue-green of the Caribbean.

The sea breeze rustled the skirt of Victoria's blue sundress. For her last day, she had dressed up to feel pretty and feminine. Lost in her gaze at the water, she felt a tug at her elbow.

"Yemaya, Yemaya es mi Santa."

An old lady was trying to tell her something through a toothless smile. When Victoria shook her head, the woman took her by the hand and led her through faded Havana streets, lined with crumbling buildings that somehow maintained their dignity. Victoria had often heard whispers of "Yemaya" as she passed but never understood.

Stopping at a large heavy wooden door, the woman let go of Victoria's hand in order to push it open, releasing a sharp smell of the sea. Victoria could not see anything until her eyes adjusted to the dark interior. The room was like a pirate's treasure trove but instead of gold and silver, it contained objects from the sea. Large woven barrels contained shells, pearls and different shades of coral. Strands of dried seaweed draped the walls.

"Yemaya," repeated the old lady, taking Victoria's hand again and dragging her towards a counter at the back of the room where a man dressed in crisp white cotton stood smiling. The counter displayed several female statues on folds of blue satin. Some were made of a light metal like tin, decorated with shell and wave like designs. Others were of a highly polished heavy black wood. There was one in the middle carved of a light green-blue stone on a silver stand with silver waves lashing up.

"Yemaya," the woman said as she pushed her closer to the statues.

The man, sensing her attraction to the turquoise one, picked it up and held it out to her.

"Yemaya," he said in a deep intoxicating voice, "queda uno solo. Que estaba esperando."

Victoria stared with her big blue eyes.

"I'm sorry. I don't understand," she said.

The man took her hand and placed the statue in it.

"From Canada?" he asked.

"Ireland," she replied.

He just nodded and gestured to the statue.

"Yemaya," he said.

The old lady perked up.

"Yemaya" she said.

The man looked into Victoria's eyes and held her there. He made her feel slightly dizzy. She sensed his power but also saw his gentleness as he got out a book and pointed to a picture.

"This is Yemaya," he said pointing to the figure of a woman coming out of the sea in a blue dress, her hair flowing. She seemed to be some sort of Goddess or saint.

"Blue is my favourite colour too," commented Victoria.

Victoria looked at the statue as if in a trance.

"Yemaya," she tried softly.

The old lady was getting very excited. Victoria asked the man what the woman wanted.

"Mirta is a follower of Yemaya. She is taken with your blue clothes and wants you to give them to her."

"My clothes?" said Victoria. "But what would I wear?"

The man pointed to rows of embroidered white cotton dresses.

"Those are very cheap," he said.

Victoria shrugged and smiled.

The man led her to a changing room. Mirta, waiting at the entrance, threw her arms around Victoria when she came out. Victoria was certain to receive Yemaya's blessing.

"You look good in white," the man said.

Victoria was worried about getting to her hotel. She had to pack before leaving the next morning.

"Mirta will see you back," said the man. "But don't you want to take this beautiful lady with you?" he added passing over the turquoise statue. "It's as if she chose you."

"No, I couldn't afford it."

However, it wasn't as expensive as she had expected. She put it under her arm and left with the old woman who was wearing Victoria's clothes, too big for her small frame.

The two of them walked back along narrow streets. When they came to a crossroads, the woman Mirta started to mime dancing with someone and pointed up a large avenue. Victoria shrugged and then mimed carrying suitcases.

"Por Favor. Ven conmigo."

Mirta took Victoria's arm. They finally arrived at what looked like a bullring. Inside, there were tables around a large orchestra playing a style of music she recognised as *son*. In the middle of the arena was a flat dirt floor filled with dancers, mainly older couples with such dignity and elegance.

Mirta dragged Victoria to a group of elderly men and women sitting in a corner.

Watching people dance, she wished that she had better rhythm. 'I just wasn't born with it', she thought, noticing that she was the only white person in the large arena. Mirta came back, excited, with a man in tow.

"El habla inglés," she said.

"Mirta has really taken to you," he said.

"Yes, I wish we could understand each other more."

"She's something special," he said shaking his head.

"Are you her husband?" asked Victoria.

The man took his time in answering.

"Admirer," he said

The man asked the typical questions. Then she did the same.

"Where did you learn your English?"

"From films," he replied.

"From films?"

"Yes, I've seen a lot of them. I work in films. I direct."

Victoria was astounded. The man had no pretensions. In Ireland a film director would be putting on airs.

"Cuba found oil off the coast. Before that we had sugar that we traded."

Victoria nodded. 'He's going to give me a history lesson', she thought. "I already went to the revolution museum."

"Before we made lots of movies. When help from Russia ended, we had no raw film. So, I make music videos now. Would you like to dance?" he asked.

"I can't," said Victoria.

"Everyone can dance," he said kindly, taking her hand and pulling her up.

"By the way, my name is Octavio. Just follow me," he said as he led her to the middle of the dance-floor.

To her surprise, Victoria felt the rhythm. The demented elephant had fled her and she was sensuous and smooth. Perhaps it was the music, a rich steady beat, no rush, no pressure. It certainly had a lot to do with this man and how she relaxed into his lead.

The woman Mirta was waiting for them when they finished.

"Ven a mi casa a comer," she said.

They all squeezed into a taxi. As she served the food, Mirta caught the hem of her new blue dress, Victoria's old one, and flapped it in front and in back, ending with a twirl. She gestured to Victoria.

"Bailles bien."

Octavio, noticing Victoria's confused expression, translated for her.

"She said you dance well," he told her.

"Thank you," Victoria said to Mirta.

"Yo no," said Mirta. "Da gracias a Yemaya."

She pulled the blue fabric of the dress up and rubbed it against her face.

"Yemaya," she said.

THE WIND THROWS
IT BACK

"Get in here, Martin." He could hear his father shout through the closed window.

No one could accuse his father of speaking too softly. His mother, God Rest her Soul, always said that there was no ignoring him. He called attention to himself from both God and the Devil. There was no telling how it would turn out in the end.

His father looked him over when he entered the room. No smile, no handshake. He hadn't seen his father for well on a year, yet he still jumped to do his every command.

"And how's Martin?" he asked.

"Not bad," Martin responded. "And how's yourself?"

"I'm all right."

His father had been in England for six years. He left Ireland after his first wife, Martin's mother, died.

"Mindy?"

Father and son looked at each other searchingly as if in a staring contest. His father looked away first.

"She's all right. Pregnant," he said.

"Figures," said Martin under his breath.

His father caught him or at least picked up the tone.

"What did you say?" he boomed.

"I said that's great."

Martin's father didn't push it. He knew there was soreness in the family that he had remarried so soon after his first wife had died. But Mindy had mended his shattered heart. He'd have to go easy. Martin was the youngest, the baby.

"And how's England?" Martin asked.

"It's not like here," his father replied, stroking his hands over his belly and coughing hard.

Martin looked away and waited. The huge framed picture of the Sacred Heart loomed above him in garish colours. Around it, covering every possible wall space were blown-up photographs of his family and ancestors. In black and white, most were taken on their wedding days, serious faces that didn't suit the occasion. His parents were up there staring straight ahead of themselves. They looked even younger than Martin did now. His eyes strayed over to his father. He hadn't changed much from the picture; had just made the transition from boy to man.

There was a flash of light.

"I'd better take another. I don't want everyone in London to think that you go around with your mouth hanging open."

Martin couldn't help himself. He started posing, subtly at first and then going into slightly more exaggerated movements.

"Always acting the idiot!" his father grunted. Stay still, look straight ahead and be serious." His father took the last photo and Martin wondered what kind of sentence he was in for.

"I've found a girl for you," his father said, and Martin felt as if his heart were nailed into the wall along with all the serious faces.

His grandmother came in with some tea and a plate of Fig Newtons, the only biscuit she could eat since she contracted diabetes several years ago. She put the tray on a small table near the sofa and sat down beside Martin, all the while keeping her eyes on his father.

"Have you told him, Dan?"

The father remained standing.

"I have, Theresa. I've just taken his picture. I'll send it off to England tomorrow."

"And do I get to see a picture too?" asked Martin.

Dan laughed. "Only if you get on the short list. She's in great demand that one."

His grandmother shook her head.

"You promised that the boy could stay with me," she argued. "When I lost my Maire and you went away, you told me you would never take the boy."

"He is a man now. You have to let him go," he said.

"He's too young." His grandmother poured the tea without looking at him.

Dan downed his cup and walked out the door mumbling that he had things to do. They heard the door slam.

Martin always joined the older lads as they drove around with carts on the back of their bicycles picking up scraps of metal they could then sell on. He knew a lot about metal. He used to watch the old ones work with it when he was small.

His grandmother came out as he was wheeling his

bicycle out the driveway of their small terraced home. It was at the end of a row and had a small yard at the side and in the back. 'The best view in town' her late husband used to say. Although it was local authority housing, it was on a hill with the town on one side and a wild field on the other. You could see the hills of Clare over to Connemara in a sweep. Grandmother Theresa didn't often leave the confines of her house and had forgotten how beautiful it was outside.

The Pomeranian dog, usually curled up in the rocking chair just inside the entrance, heard the old woman outside and scratched to get out. Grandmother Theresa opened the door a crack and felt the dog at her heels.

"Martin, you'll be back for your tea."

"I'll be back," said Martin.

"We'll try to keep you here," she called after him. "It's not right to take you away from here."

Martin, out of hearing range, smiled and waved.

* * *

Martin followed his mate Ronnie back to the centre of town. They parked their bikes outside a house with a long drive. Ronnie knocked and a lady came to the door and led them around back to the shed. Through the open door she pointed to a line of old paint cans on shelves along the side.

After Ronnie and Martin loaded the cans onto their carts, they went up to the house again to collect their money. Ronnie then brought him to a bushy area of the canal. They leaned their bikes against a wall and sat looking down at the water, legs dangling over the side. Ronnie rolled a cigarette, lit it and inhaled deeply.

When he finished, Ronnie told Martin that they'd better finish the job. He walked over to the bicycle cart, grabbed a couple of paint cans and threw them into the canal. They were slow to sink.

"C'mon Martin. We'd better hurry up."

But Martin stayed where he was.

"Wait. There's a place for those," he argued.

Ronnie said that it would be too much trouble. "No one will know if we do it quickly," he said.

Martin still hesitated. "I fish here in the summer."

"It's just a few cans." Ronnie yawned.

"Paint cans," said Martin. "I bring the fish home and my grandmother cooks them for us."

Ronnie was going to throw them in anyway so in the end he thought that he might as well get it over with.

They separated at the crossroads and Martin kept thinking of fish coming out of his mouth, a strange expression on their 'faces', each one a different colour.

"I'm home, Gran," he said.

"What kept you?" she called from the kitchen.

"Just some things I had to do. Where's my da?"

"He had some things to do. Men! You're all the same."

Martin smiled. "I'm starving. What's for tea?"

"Fish."

The Pomeranian stood under the kitchen table to receive offerings from Martin's dinner plate. Dan arrived home long after they finished eating, his face red from exertion. Loud incessant barking could be heard from the back shed and the Pomeranian joined the chorus.

"What's that racket?" asked Grandmother Theresa.

"I bought two dogs. Going to fight them. Just leave them out there. I'm going back to England tomorrow but I'll be back."

"What are their names?" asked Martin.

Dan's face got redder.

"They are not fuckin' pets. Can you not get it through that thick skull of yours? They're fighting dogs."

"We'll look after them when you are gone," said Grandmother Theresa.

"Just leave them alone I said."

"But we'll have to feed them. They'll starve." Martin opened the fridge to see if there was anything he could give them.

"That's what I want. Them nice and hungry. Now leave them alone, I'm warning you."

Dan then got up and said he was going out for a jar. Over the barking, they heard a door slam.

Grandmother Theresa was sitting in her worn armchair when Martin came down to his breakfast. He gestured to her to stay where she was.

"He's gone back," she sighed.

Martin nodded, buttered a piece of bread, found a few sausages in the pan and leaned against the wall eating. The Pomeranian slid off its chair to place itself in a position to pick up anything that fell. The sound of barking could be still heard in the shed but was weaker and not as continuous.

He took up the remaining sausages from the pan and a bowl of potatoes from last night's dinner and went out the back door, not noticing the shock of the Pomeranian as the door closed behind him. Martin stayed outside the shed for a long time and whistled a few tunes to get the dogs accustomed to him before addressing them in soft murmurs. The barking quietened. Martin slowly lifted the latch and opened the door a crack, still whispering and calming. He squeezed himself inside and gently closed the door, a prickle of fear rising up for a moment as he realised he was enclosed in a small space with unknown beasts.

Their heads hung down as they watched him from eyes that seemed too large for the tiny, slim heads. Muscles twitched on their bodies. Not an inch of fat. Tails moved tentatively. Martin wanted to run his hand along their sleek forms. He had not been this close to purebred greyhounds before. He emptied the food onto an old newspaper.

At lunchtime Martin grabbed his bike and cycled into town. He went to the backdoor of restaurants asking for scraps for the dogs. Some were happy to see him carry away bags of waste; others told him not to bother them again.

The dogs were quiet when he arrived in the back garden. Curled up at the back of the shed, they pricked up their ears when he came in. He made soothing sounds again and braved a brief pat on the head of one of them.

Late back to school again, Martin realised that he had not had anything to eat himself. As soon as the last bell rang, he raced for his bike and made it home in record time. Grandmother was still having a nap upstairs so he quickly coated a couple of slices of bread with jam and rushed off to join Ronnie and the others along the river by the university where they searched the large skips behind new buildings in search of scrap metal. Martin didn't stick around with the lads after they were finished.

"I've got things to do," he said.

The dogs were waiting for him this time. With the same familiar noises and whistling, Martin knelt down, put out his hand and lightly stroked the side of one of them. The skin was soft, strong muscles underneath, ready to run. He made a loop in a rope and put it around the neck of the closest dog. He did the same with the other. Gripping the end of the ropes, he guided them up to the field on the hill.

Martin wasn't sure if they'd come to him if they were let free but the kind of exercise he could give them on the lead was quite different from a good run. He let them go. They bounded off and Martin could feel their happiness. It was contagious.

With the food and exercise, the dogs were getting stronger and even more beautiful. Martin would have loved them even if they didn't run so fast. But to see them race like the wind, made his heart jump!

One day, he took the dogs down to the beach. They trembled as they watched a bearded heron sitting on a rock. Martin kept them on the ropes until the bird stretched and lifted off into the air, its peace disturbed. The dogs ran after it but stopped when they got their feet wet. They didn't seem to mind running in the shallow tide near the sand but would not go further into the sea.

"C'mon girls," he called and they came to him.

Later, instead of doing homework, Martin thought up names he could give the dogs. Once he had settled on what would suit each one, he felt even more connected.

"Martin, come down. Your father is on the phone. He's ringing from over there." Grandmother Theresa called up the stairs and then went back to her chair in the kitchen, warm by the range.

Martin scrambled down the stairs. The phone was waiting for him on the table just inside the front door.

"How are ya?" he asked.

"What were you doing? Dreaming again?"

Martin didn't answer.

"Well, boy, we're in with a chance. I'd say 5-1." His father sounded cheerful for a change but Martin had no idea what he was talking about.

"What?" he asked.

"You've made the short list lad. The girl wants to meet you."

"That's great!" Martin couldn't help but sound bored, but his father didn't appear to notice this time.

"A photo is on the way. You're going to be blown away."

"Umh"

"And how're the dogs doing?" his father inquired.

"Out the back," Martin replied.

"Good lad. I'll be over for them soon."

A large brown envelope arrived from England in the post. It was addressed to Grandmother Theresa. He had just come in from the dogs' walk and saw it lying there on the floor. He walked into the kitchen and handed it to his grandmother. She took it and handed it back to him.

"Open it yourself. You know it's for you."

He ripped the envelope open and reached inside. There was a photo of a girl. Not an enlarged glossy or anything like that. It was just an ordinary photo. Looking inside to see if there was a letter or card with it and seeing there was none, he held out the photo and looked at it. She was pretty. Long dark hair, big eyes, and rosy complexion, about his age. What was the big deal? There were many girls just as pretty around home.

"Well?"

Martin handed the photo to his grandmother.

"Nice," she said.

She tried to hand it back to Martin but he shook his head.

"You keep it," he said.

On his way up to his room to do his homework, he realised he didn't even know the girl's name.

* * *

Dan slammed the front door and hollered for Martin. There was a short, stocky man with him. Grandmother came out of the kitchen with the Pomeranian at her feet. The dog took a dislike to the other gentleman and snapped at his heels causing the man to back up and lift his feet away from the dog. He looked like he was trying out a new kind of dance.

"Get off, Tiny," Dan growled as he gave the dog a kick into the kitchen.

He then turned to Grandmother Theresa.

"This is Gina's dad, like I told you. We won't be staying. We just came to get the dogs."

"Good to meet you." she said to the man. "I thought we'd be seeing your daughter here."

"You'll be seeing her soon enough." Dan told her. "Now, we have a fight on and don't want to be late. I'll just get the dogs."

Grandmother was secretly glad that the stranger was not staying with them and when she heard Dan cursing in the back garden, she was glad that he was not staying either. Although the front door opened and slammed again, she did not get up from her chair in the kitchen.

"I told Martin not to feed those god-damn mutts. I have a lot riding on them. You tell the lad that he's in big trouble. Where is he anyhow?"

When Martin came home from his bike rounds, he went right out to the shed and, not finding the dogs, tore into the kitchen.

"Where are they?" he asked.

"They're gone," said Theresa.

"Where?" he cried.

"Leave it, Martin. I don't know."

Martin pounded the kitchen table with his fists.

"He told you to leave them alone. They aren't yours."

He slammed the door on the way out and started asking around if anyone knew where a dogfight was taking place. No one could help him and time was quickly passing. A few stars glowed in the blackened sky and the night wind was up.

Bed, however, seemed somehow impossible. So he cycled around the town until the sun peeked over the barracks.

Grandmother Theresa frowned when she opened the front door to find the man who had been with Dan the previous day. Martin hadn't come home to sleep and she had hoped it was him. However, she soon lightened up when she found that the man wasn't alone.

"Gina's going to stay around for awhile and get to know you," the man said.

"Where's Dan?" Theresa asked.

"Gone back to England. Didn't do too well last night, thanks to our lad!"

She nodded solemnly and then welcomed them in.

"Martin's just doing some of his rounds. He's a hardworking lad, that one."

She brought them into the kitchen and put the kettle on.

"Not for me," the man said. "I have to go down the country. I have business. Be back for Gina in a few weeks."

He left without saying anything to his daughter and without saying goodbye to the grandmother.

The older woman shrugged as if to say, "men, who needs them?" Over tea she asked Gina to tell her about herself. As the girl talked, she almost forgot her worry about Martin.

Grandmother thought that if she heard the front door slam again, she would scream. But when she heard Martin's voice, she felt something rise in her chest.

"I'm not going to school today. I didn't find them." he called from the bottom of the stairs.

"There's hot tea," Theresa called back.

"Not now. I'm going to sleep. Up all night."

"Just come here for a minute, will you?" asked Theresa.

Martin reluctantly made for the kitchen. He was about to say he was ok and retreat up to his room. But he came face to face with a young girl, the girl in the photo.

"This is Gina," said Grandmother.

"Christ!" he said.

"Watch what you're saying, young man."

"Sorry," he said.

"Don't sorry me. I'm used to you. It's sorry to Gina! She's staying with us for a while." His grandmother smiled. "I hope you'll show her around," she said." She'll be bored with an old one like me."

Martin moved Tiny off the chair opposite Gina's and said he'd take a cup of tea but that then he had to get a bit of sleep. The two young people stared at each other without saying a word. Then he got up, put his teacup on the counter and went upstairs to bed. When he came down, Gina was waiting for him.

"Where are you going to take me this afternoon?"

"I have to meet the lads and do a few jobs."

"Can I come?" she asked. "I've hardly seen anything of this place. I'm supposed to come from here and I don't even know it."

"Sure, come if you like." Martin looked at Gina. "You talk funny."

"And so do you" she said. Martin looked away and smiled.

Martin went around and looked at the empty shed before attaching the cart to his bicycle and helping Gina onto the bar in front of him. They raced along the road, Gina howling with delight. The lads were waiting behind the hospital.

"Who's that?" asked Ronnie.

Martin shrugged. "A friend of the family's over from England ."

The job was to take bags from the hospital to the dump. They wouldn't just toss them anywhere this time. There was too much. Each of them would have his cart loaded to capacity. Martin went to help bring out the bags.

When they were finished, they started off on the long cycle to the dump. The load in the carts was heavy and the journey was slow. It was especially hard for Martin with Gina on the front. But he didn't say anything.

The little convoy arrived at the dump. Martin suggested Gina stay at the entrance as she was gagging from the smell. The lads, used to it, drove close to one of the piles and started hurling bags onto it. They were almost finished when Ronnie nudged Martin.

"It's just as well your one didn't come. I think I see something moving there."

They all laughed but as Martin looked at the pile expecting to see a rat, his face dropped. The 'moving' thing was a dog, or what was left of one. He was frightened to approach it, frightened at what it had become. It lay there, large raw gaping wounds, its face half off, barely recognisable.

With a deep breath, Martin approached the animal

making the comforting noises he had made when he was getting to know the greyhounds. The dog was quiet now, breathing shallowly. It had made a tremendous effort when it heard Martin's voice. Then it lay still again. Martin bent down and touched it lightly.

"It's ok girl. It's ok," he said.

The lads approached to what was going on.

"She's my dog," said Martin. "And there might be another one around here."

They split up and combed the pile.

"Over here," called Jackie.

Martin left one dog's side and found the other in worse condition. He put his ear to her smooth chest and heard a faint beating.

The lads found lengths of cloth: old curtains, sheets, horse blankets. They weren't exactly clean but the priority was to get the animals out of that place. The lads lifted the dogs onto the carts. Promising to go slowly, they told Martin they would meet them at the house. Gina was a bit confused until, back at the house, Martin told his grandmother what he had found at the dump. She sent them back the shed and proceeded to boil water and herbs to clean the wounds.

"Martin, listen to me," she said. "I don't know if I will be able to do anything. They seem very bad."

Martin looked at the ground.

"Martin, listen to me."

"I know. But we have to try."

Gina piped up. "I think you should take them to a vet."

"A vet will only put them down."

"That's so they won't suffer too much when there's nothing you can do."

"But there is. Gran is great when it comes to making things better.

Waiting with the dogs in the shed, he thought back to the days when they were strong vibrant creatures until Theresa came carrying water, disinfectant and her mixture of herbs to help the wounds heal.

She first went to work on the dog that was not as bad off. While Martin soothed the dog, she cleansed the wound, applied disinfectant and covered the sore in geranium leaves. Then Gina passed towels soaked in a solution of boiled blackberry leaves, which the woman pressed gently over the wounds and bound them with a clean strip of torn sheet.

"This one's bad," she said looking at the second dog.

Martin couldn't talk.

"Watch me carefully. This process has to be repeated three times a day in the beginning," said Grandmother. "Until healing begins."

"We'll have to get more old cloths," Martin managed.

Grandmother shook her head.

"I have more than enough sheets, towels and blankets than I can ever use. People keep giving me sheets. For some reason they think I like or need them."

Martin helped her up when she finished. The dogs had winced with pain when the disinfectant was applied and they were whining softly.

"Come in the house 'til I give you some blankets to put over them."

Gina put the dirty cloths in the bucket and followed her. Once inside, she took the bucket from Gina.

"We'll burn these," she said.

Grandmother Theresa sent out some extra blankets because she knew that Martin wouldn't be leaving the dogs. She also sent some bread and a bit of bacon for him to eat. When Gina arrived back at the shed, Martin was soothing first one dog and then the other.

"I'm staying too," said Gina.

* * *

Martin opened an eye and for a moment wondered where he was. He had formed his body around the sleeping back of one of the dogs and Gina had done the same with the other dog. She was still asleep and her hair was loose, hanging over the dog. Martin didn't know why he didn't think her beautiful before.

Listening to the sounds of the day – birds, cars in the distance, building work – Martin knew that it was later than when he usually woke up. School seemed like something far away. He went out in the back garden to take a leak.

"Martin," called Gina. "Are you there?" "You have to come here," she said.

Martin knelt down beside her.

"Feel her," she said. "She's cold and stiff."

Martin felt the dog and put his ear to her chest.

"It is good you were near her at the end," he choked.

They wrapped her tightly in a blanket and put her under the back porch while they carried out Grandmother Theresa's instructions on the other dog. The lads came by in the afternoon and helped them dig a grave in the top field where the dogs had enjoyed running.

Martin continued to sleep with the dog but Gina moved into the house. After a week Grandmother came out to the shed to examine the animal.

"It's time to go back to school," she said.

"But ..."

"No buts," said Theresa. "The dog is better. Gina and I can look after it."

So Martin went back to school and even helped the lads out a bit. But as soon as he got home, he was in the shed with the dog. He would find Gina there.

"Don't you go to school?" he asked.

"I can catch up," she replied.

The dog was getting better. In a while she struggled to get up. Theresa had a look before Martin would let her stand and go out to the garden to do her business.

"She's very scarred," said Gina.

"Aren't we all in someway? She's lucky to be alive."

Slowly the dog got strong enough to go to the top field again and to start running a little bit at a time.

Martin moved into the house. He was in his room when the phone rang.

"I'm never answering that thing again," he called down and let it ring. Grandmother scolded him as she lifted herself out of her chair and caught it just in time.

"It could be important," she said.

It was Gina's father. He'd meet her at the bus station. They were going back to England.

Martin walked out, took the dog out of the shed and brought it to the top field. This time he let it go wherever it wanted. It took off into a run that it hadn't done since it was hurt. It seemed to run for its pain, for its dead sister, for its whole breed. Martin was so entranced that he didn't hear Gina come up behind him.

"Will it come back?" asked Gina

"It will come back," said Martin. He edged closer to her and put his arm around her.

"You know, you are truly lovely," he said, pulling her closer and touching her lips with his own.

When they opened their eyes, they saw the greyhound bounding for them at full speed. Jumping up on them, they fell to the ground, laughing. The dog began licking their faces.

"We'll be married then?" He was tentative but gained confidence as he went on. "Then no one will be able to tell us what to do."

After dinner, Gina got out her Polaroid camera and had Grandmother take their photo with the dog. Martin got an old frame from the attic and hung their picture on the sitting room wall with all the family pictures. Grandmother wasn't sure it was the right place for it, but Martin insisted.

"I love you," he whispered to Gina.

"I love you too," she whispered back.

The next morning, as she was leaving, Gina put down her suitcase to look at the photo.

"At least we look happy," she said.

He carried out her bags to the taxi.

"Alive is the word. We look alive."

Note: *Arranged marriages are still common among the Irish Traveller Community*

FOR THE MONEY

"I just do it for the money," said Kevin.

Coffee smelled good and whipped him into the kind of shape that he could function in. Served him right for thinking he could drink like he did twenty years ago. Funny how he reverted back to that time just because his friend Gerry had turned up after twenty years without any contact. Gerry looked great this morning.

Kevin, on the other hand had a head that felt like it might explode and he didn't dare look in the mirror. He knew exactly what he would see – bags under the eyes, stubble-chin, pasty coloured skin and tossed hair. His mouth felt dry and tasted of smoke, odd since he had given up cigarettes more than three years ago.

"Was I smoking last night?" he asked.

Gerry pointed to a dirty ashtray on the coffee table.

"We ended up in the smoking room at the Cuban Embassy: the finest cigars, good rum and great party people. You did a mean salsa!"

Kevin hit the sides of his head with his hands.

"Ouch."

"You don't remember, do you?" Gerry teased.

Adjusting the lilac tie that went with his steel grey suit, Gerry took another sip of coffee.

"I can't believe what you said – that you just do it for the money."

Kevin shrugged.

"We have to make a living somehow," he said.

"Yeah," said Gerry, "but it's always nicer if you like what you're doing. You have always loved journalism."

"Well, I love a lot of things. I love staying in bed late. I love having time to watch people. Read books. Spend time with friends. It doesn't mean those things have to be my job."

Kevin walked over to the kitchen counter, pulled open a drawer and took out a packet of Rothmans and a lighter.

"Feck," he said, "over three bloody years down the tube. All for nothing."

Walking back to his seat beside Gerry, he pointed to his belly.

"This is what I got for it. Giving up the smokes wasn't so bad. But this just appeared in a month."

"You don't have to do it. You can stop." Gerry reached out his arm for Kevin to pass over the cigarettes.

"I did stop."

"And you can do it again."

Kevin lit up. After a long drag, he felt light-headed.

"You sure I was smoking last night?"

Gerry left to go to a conference at the Foreign Affairs Ministry. Now a diplomat, he had given up his job as journalist to travel the world. He had studied with Kevin, worked with Kevin on the paper and swore he missed it like hell. But Kevin knew differently. Gerry was lucky to have got out when he did. Shortly after he left, the paper had had a, what was the expression, 'a downsizing of its staff'. Kevin was on the list. Hard times until he built up a sizable freelance market. The problem was that half of the time he put into work was spent hustling. He had to chase down money, push ideas for stories, ask banks for money. He hated it all. He just wanted to write.

The shower felt good but Kevin didn't bother to shave. He made a pot of coffee and took it up the windy stairs to the attic where he had his office. Sitting at his desk, finishing his third cup, he cursed deadlines. He had to make yet another meeting sound interesting. The Celtic Tiger had produced an endless stream of these experiments in working together. Everyone was talking. Working towards a new and better ... ah well. He was just cynical, the plague of all journalists.

The afternoon sun lit up the clock on the bookcase. Four o'clock. Gerry had told him to turn on the television at that time to catch an interview with the Arab leader Mujadi. Afterwards, there was Gerry waffling on as an expert on the Middle East. That was Gerry – always good with the talk, the serious look, the discreet smile, the subtle hand gestures. Yes, there he was looking impeccable, people eating out of his hand. Saying feck all. Fair play to him anyway. Kevin didn't have time to dwell on it. He had a date with a deadline. He did exercises to get more oxygen to his head. Think of a good lead sentence. Ah – the drink last night didn't help.

Downstairs he poured himself a glass of wine and

wondered if he should start making dinner or if he would go out to eat with Gerry. His college friend was only in town for a few days. They had to make the most of it.

Perhaps Janie would meet them later. Janie, his girlfriend since he and Pam had broken up, was his salvation. Kevin could not believe his luck. She was young, beautiful, intelligent and fun. Things were in perspective when he was with Janie. Serious when they had to be. Light and fun at other times. Even Janie's voice on the answering machine made him feel better about life – a sexy voice: "This is Janie. But I can't be reached at the moment. Leave a message."

He poured another glass of wine and grabbed the phone when it rang. It was Gerry, not Janie. A table was booked at a good restaurant in town.

"Oh and Kevin, I was wondering if you might put on a suit and tie," he said. "Other people might be joining us."

Working at home, Kevin had been out of the suit scene for years. He squeezed into his dark blue one, having gained a few pounds since he had last worn it. He had put it away after his last job interview when he vowed he'd never go through that again. He would work for himself.

After trying on several ties, he decided to go without. Better to look underdressed than hideous.

When he arrived at the restaurant, Gerry was sitting at a table full of men in suits. Kevin was disappointed. He had hoped to have his friend to himself.

The men stood up.

"Kevin, you know the Minister?" Gerry gestured to a small round-headed man at his side.

"Nice to meet you." Kevin put out his hand.

The chat dealt with affairs of the state since that was in the world in which most of the diners were submerged. There were also jokes, comments about football and personal anecdotes. The Minister showed an interest in what Kevin was doing. Contrary to what Kevin had expected, it wasn't such an ordeal. They were all good sports and not unlikeable, not overtly artificial.

The Minister and his entourage left after coffee. Kevin and Gerry stayed on, ordering another bottle of wine. The two friends together! Each story from college sparked another one.

Finally, Gerry poured the last of the bottle, held up his glass and toasted Kevin.

"I think I've got you a new job," he said. Kevin looked at him and laughed.

"No, seriously. They want another body in Abu Dhabi and I recommended you," he said, adding: "The Minister liked you."

Kevin was still laughing but he saw that his friend's face was serious. He was going to blurt something out but decided to be diplomatic for a change.

"I don't know what to say," he said. Diplomacy wasn't as easy as he thought.

Gerry broke into a smile from across the table.

"It means we can be together, pal. We'll have a great time. Just like the old days."

Kevin emptied his glass and seeing there was no more wine, poured some water from the pitcher.

"I know that you have gone to a lot of trouble," he said. "But I have work here, I have a life."

Gerry nodded.

"Truthfully Kevin, it's not as if you are making the earth shake. It's nice to make a difference."

Angry, Kevin tried another tact.

"Just because you sold out, Gerry ... You gave up journalism for the diplomatic corps – just another glorified PR job."

Gerry remained calm. Looking Kevin in the eye, he said:

"You told me yourself. You are just in it for the money."

"If you believed that, you're ... What money?"

Then Kevin suddenly stopped protesting and agreed that there was little enjoyment in the articles he was churning out at that moment.

"And," said Gerry, "it would mean such a better lifestyle."

"Tell me more."

"You'll never have to carry an umbrella again."

"And the drink?"

"At the embassies, there's always drink."

Gerry ordered a bottle of champagne and was toasting their new life, together again. In truth there was little Kevin would miss. Then he remembered Janie – the way she burst into song, the way sunlight caught on her ginger lashes, her soft skin.

Gerry seemed to read his thoughts.

"There are plenty of girls over there."

"I couldn't leave Janie," Kevin said firmly. He had been caught up in his friend's words. The life he was weaving was not what he wanted.

Gerry covered his hand with his.

"I guess you don't remember last night."

"What about last night? Kevin turned pale.

"We were talking about our college days and all the girls we knew. Remember Marta, the Cuban or that contortionist?"

Kevin got impatient. "Yeah, yeah. What happened?"

"We thought Janie was in the next room asleep but she was listening to everything. She came into the kitchen and called you a fecker and said she never wanted to see you again."

Kevin groaned.

"She wouldn't even wait for us to call a cab. Said she'd grab one on the street."

The champagne suddenly looked dull and unappetising. Kevin stared at the tablecloth while Gerry took a phone call. Diplomatic as ever, he told Kevin that it appeared that there wouldn't be another post after all.

"No money," he said. But Kevin feared he had not come up to scratch with the Minister.

They were quiet in the taxi back to the house. Kevin tried phoning Janie's mobile but she didn't answer. When he texted her, she replied, "Piss Off." He could hardly wait until the next morning when Gerry would be gone. Kevin wanted him to disappear now, pronto. Immediately.

But he took a long drag of his cigarette – he was getting to like them again – and decided that he could be diplomatic one more time.

"It was so good seeing you again, Gerry." He put out his hand. "We must do it again soon.

GORSE FIRES

The smoke had a sweet acrid smell, unique to burning turf. Through the window she could see flames spreading fast through the dry summer bog. Her heart pounded as she dialled.

"Maisie Kelly here. There's a fire on the bog out near my place. I'm scared of my life that it will come up to the house and burn me out."

The local fire department worked hard to put out the fire. Later the two men filed into Maisie's kitchen. She placed a mug of tea in front of each of them and put a plate of scones on the table. A mixture of ash and dirt streaked the firemen's faces.

"That was a close one."

Johnsie took a big gulp of tea and reached for a biscuit.

"If the wind was any stronger, the house would have gone," Peter said, "What do you think started it?"

"Anything could have sparked it off. With the bog so dry this summer, it's like kindling."

Peter wiped ash off his face. "There's usually been enough rain."

"Just goes to show you," said Johnsie, "how fast it can dry up and turn brittle and parched. Fire then spreads like wildfire."

"What's wildfire anyway?"

"I don't know. It's just an expression."

Maisie came over with some more scones and hot tea.

"I'd say you got a great shock, Maisie," said Johnsie. "It was a good thing you were here. You could have come back to a pile of blackened stones. Isn't that right Peter?"

The other man nodded and slumped down in his chair. Johnsie put down his cup and jumped to his feet.

"Well, Maisie, that was a great cup of tea. But we'd better be getting back now. Are you all right?"

Maisie sighed. "I'm fine."

It was a pleasant drive back to the fire station through the bog with its many deep lakes and the sun shining. Peter hadn't been on the bog road for six months and he realised that he had missed it. The land! It gets under your skin and becomes part of you.

"Well," teased Johnsie. "Is that the first time you have been out there since?"

"It is."

"She's still mad about you, you know."

"It's over."

Johnsie looked out the window at the radio tower in the distance.

"She's a good-looking woman."

"I know."

"Well, then why did you break up?"

"I guess I just wanted some space."

The two men lapsed into silence until they arrived back at the station. They showered and changed, filled the water tanks on the engine and checked that everything was ready to go.

* * *

Sun streamed through the windows of Maisie's workroom, catching on the coloured glass pieces and turning the walls into a wild painting of violet, turquoise and yellow. A piece of crimson glass lay on the table in front of her. She took up the cutting tool and formed an arch type shape, part of a window commissioned for an old hotel that was being done up.

It had been wonderful seeing Peter again. It seemed like such a long time since they had broken up. She still remembered the last sentence he shouted before slamming the door and driving away. "I'm suffocating out here," he'd said.

Out of a pale green piece of glass, she cut a circle to make into an apple. The hotel had wanted a fruit motif to represent abundance. But she was adding in local bits. Oversized blackberries, bog cotton bent in the wind, a background of colours of the bog: russets, dark greens, earthy browns and soft heather blues, pinks and purples. Cutting out the leaves to go with the apple, Maisie pressed down too hard with the knife and glass splintered into tiny pieces, cutting her. Red blood dripped down the green glass.

* * *

The dry period held out. Uncharacteristically, there was no rain for weeks. Instead of enjoying it, the locals became worried.

"What's happened to our weather?" they said. Many couldn't sleep at night for the heat. Towns started rationing water. Left unwashed, cars took on the reckless dusty look of southern cousins.

The large windows in Maisie's workroom looked over a wild expanse of bog and rock and a few scattered piles of stone ruins. Strong sunlight hit the glass she was working on and burned. Maisie had heard the story of a man that came home from work one day to find his bed on fire. There had been no one in the house. He didn't smoke so did not drop a match down the mattress. Flames just came out of the middle of the bed for no apparent reason. The fire chief knew right away. He picked up a small hand mirror the man's girlfriend had left on a side table. 'There's the culprit,' he said, explaining how the hot sun had hit the mirror and bounced off on to the bed, causing it to catch fire.

Maisie covered all the windows in old sheets. No longer was the beautiful endless bog on view; she felt closed in and isolated.

* * *

There was an old building in the village that Maisie had her eye on to use as a studio. Although it was left abandoned after the old man who lived there died, there was a dispute among his descendants. If Maisie could only rent the building! No one liked to go out to take classes or visit where she was now. It was too out of the way.

Cian Tully looked after the property. A bachelor, he lived over the shop on the main street.

"Ah, Maisie, now you're lucky you caught me. I'm just back for the extension lead. We're working on Patsy Murray's new house."

"Do you have a minute?"

"Well, he's not getting married 'til October. So I guess it can wait a few moments."

In the end Cian told Maisie she could have the old building for a minimal rent.

Just then, a siren screeched by. They ran out to see the tail-end of a fire truck turn into the old bog road.

"It must be close to your place."

Maisie ran to her car.

"I'll follow you out there."

Once they turned off the main road, they could see clouds of smoke across the bog in the distance. Maisie raced down the road to her house. The fire was near. She could see the flames, and after jumping out of her car, could feel the heat. Without even closing the car door, she ran onto the bog towards the firemen.

"Go back, Maisie. It's not safe," someone shouted. She thought she recognised Johnsie's voice. "Go back and phone for more help."

* * *

Neighbours kept arriving. Peter organised a group of men to dig a trench so the fire couldn't spread. The backbreaking work eventually paid off. The fire was eventually contained and put out.

"Did you smell petrol?" Peter asked Johnsie.

"Yeah, I think I did."

Back at the house Maisie was rushing around making everyone tea. Taking a batch of biscuits out of the oven, she bumped into Johnsie.

"You okay?"

"Fine."

"Maisie, did you see anyone out on the bog?"

"No, there's never anybody. You know yourself."

Johnsie pulled her over to the door where they could be alone.

"I'm only asking because we think there was a smell of petrol."

"Petrol?"

"We think someone might have deliberately set it."

"That's absurd," she said loudly.

Johnsie didn't want to worry the rest of the people.

"That's the second time the bog went on fire," said one man.

"We should have someone watching all the time," another added.

An old man in a tattered jacket stood up.

"I'm worried about my boat."

The neighbours decided to call a public meeting and invite the Government Minister.

* * *

The fire chief was under pressure from the minister to find out the cause of the fires.

"Don't you think it a bit strange that these fires were out where you used to live?" he asked Peter.

"Fire can strike anywhere, anytime," he responded.

"The minister told me there was smell of petrol."

"There was a faint smell."

The chief told Peter to sit down. He outlined the expense of the fires and the worry they were causing the locals. Even though the fire department was exempt from the water rationing, they had to be careful.

"I understand that sir," Peter said.

"Then can you guarantee that your girlfriend isn't setting the fires?"

"What?"

"Someone told me that she had gone a bit batty lately."

"What she does is none of your business!"

"It's my business if she's setting fires. Not your fault," said the Chief, "but I'm going to have to give you a leave of absence until this blows over."

"Fine." Peter was getting angry. "As long as I'm paid."

The chief got up and walked out of the room without saying goodbye. Peter didn't feel much like saying goodbye to anyone either. He walked out of the fire station, into the travel agent and booked a holiday to the Canary Islands for two weeks. May as well take advantage.

* * *

Maisie had a quick shower to get rid of the petrol smell. While out in the bog, some of the gas had spilled on her. After changing her dress, she took a bottle of wine out of the fridge and wandered into her workroom, now empty-looking after her move to the village. The sheet-draped windows gave a muted watery effect. Stagnant heat tinged the air. Maisie pulled down the sheets revealing the bog she loved so much. In the distance smoke was already creeping low against the dry land and beginning to billow out into the cloudless sky.

Dragging an old armchair over to the window, Maisie poured herself a glass of wine and settled down to watch the fire. She wouldn't phone this time!

Closing her eyes, Maisie imagined the tiny frogs she had seen leaping in the bog, the black beetles and her beloved bog cotton. She recalled the subtle changes on her long daily walks. Sometimes a dog followed her; other times a bird swept over her head, screeching into the silence.

The smoke crept nearer to the house, surrounding her with the tangy scent of peat. Flames shimmied up against the walls and turf smoke entered the room like incense.

***

"Cian, I hear that Maisie's going to move in with you when she gets out of the hospital."

The family of old Hedderman had given him a good price on the old house that Maisie was renting as a studio. Cian planned to make it habitable. In the meantime, he had done up a room in his flat for her.

"Is there anything in the rumours that she set it herself?"

"You know how they talk around here. I was the one who found her. The smoke crept up on her like a thief and put her to sleep before she had time to call the station."

The day Maisie came out of hospital, clouds started

forming again in the sky. She knew she was lucky to have survived. Doctors had wanted her to stay for psychiatric observation but Cian had convinced them that he would take good care of her. By the time they were half way to the village, clouds had joined together into an angry gray mass and drops splashed onto the windscreen. Getting out of the car, Maisie put her face up to the rain as it soaked the bog. The water formed tiny lakes; it wound through crevices and brought life to the burnt earth.

CONTAMINATED HEART

"We can't afford you but we need you," was how the young city councillor greeted her. "We're expecting a lot."

Not only did Sharon feel unwelcome, she was immediately thrown to the feeding frenzy of the press. The city hall conference room was full of journalists who appeared ready for the kill. Used to fighting both government agencies and the media, however, she was well able to handle them.

"We'll be doing all in our power to find the source of the contamination. I assure you I will be working day and night with city officials. In the meantime, continue to boil your water."

What was it with Councillor Duff? He'd sat next to her the whole time but left it up to her to field all the tough questions. 'Politicians! Always the same. Passing the buck,' she thought.

She was so busy answering that she hardly got a look at the councillor. Glancing at him now, she noticed he was attractive, tall, strongly built. From her research into the city's water problem, she'd read that Jim Duff was the most eligible bachelor in the city. No doubt he would stay that way with such a nasty personality.

Sitting back to collect her thoughts before taking another question, she noticed the bottles of spring water on the table and poured herself a glass.

A camera flashed in her face, blinding her for a moment. It made her realise how tired she was. She had flown to the capital that morning, rented a car and had hardly had a break until she arrived in the city for the press conference.

There had been only one stop. Entering the county, there were two quaint village pubs side by side. She had a sandwich and tea in one that was dark and wood-lined and when she got up to pay, she noticed large containers of water behind the bar.

"Are you affected the same way as the city? The water I mean."

"No, we have the other yoke," the old man behind the bar replied. "The e-coli. Been boiling our water for years."

Another question from a journalist brought Sharon back to the conference at city hall.

"Dr. McLaughlin, what is the time frame for finding a solution?"

"Well, although I have been informed of the situation, I've only just arrived. I'll be starting on the problem first thing in the morning," Sharon said. "I will be issuing regular reports."

"But when?"

"We all agree the sooner the better. Let's leave it there for now."

After settling into her hotel room, Sharon went down to the pool and swam her daily lengths. Tempted by the spa, she soaked up the heat in a room with light therapy and a fountain. She felt soothed by the sound of the water and her mind drifted back to the desert, where she had worked to find water and create irrigation systems. Fountains in those areas were a pleasure beyond comparison.

A maid came to her room to deliver bottles of spring water and reminded Sharon not to use the tap water, not even to brush her teeth. The advice wasn't necessary. Sharon knew everything about water. She had made a list of facts she knew about the city. The sewage treatment plant had been in operation for ten years. Since that time all the local beaches had received a safe blue flag. She pulled back the curtains and looked out onto the tiny medieval streets of the city centre. 'Medieval,' she repeated to herself. 'Perhaps it's the pipes.'

The next morning, she rushed to city hall to get a map showing the location of all the old lead pipes still in use.

"You'll have a time of it figuring them out. Many of the old ones, we don't know where they go at all. It's like a puzzle. I suppose they all fit together somehow."

Sharon shivered. In other locations she had had to descend into the sewers to see where pipes went in order to look for leaks. She hoped she wouldn't have to do this here.

"Councillor Duff will certainly be relieved if you find something," said the engineer as he passed over the plans.

"He's not very friendly, is he?"

"Not friendly? He's one of the nicest people I know. He is beside himself with worry over this water situation. You can't have a city of eighty thousand with no clean water. Not to mention the tourists. "

Sharon brought the plans over to a clear counter and laid them out. She was studying them when Jim Duff walked in.

"Found anything yet?"

"Give me a chance. It's my first day on the job. And you really threw me into it yesterday. I hadn't even officially started."

His face, although still showing the strain of worry, took on a gentler expression.

"Sorry. It's just that people are desperate to have safe water."

"Wait, what's this building? There are pipes dating back centuries here. I'd like to have a look."

"It's called The River Tower. It was there to keep a record of fisheries. It's not used now except for storing old bits of rope and things like that."

"Well, I'll start there anyway. See where these old pipes go."

The councillor arranged to get her keys to the building and drove her up to the entrance.

"I have a meeting. But be sure to phone me if you find anything."

"I don't have a mobile with me."

"It's not far from your hotel. Ring from there."

His arm brushed against hers as he opened the car door to let her out. Sharon felt a spark of heat course through her.

"Good luck," he called as he drove away.

The gate to the tower walkway, a rickety wooden footbridge, was secured with a rusty padlock. Sharon struggled to open it, bracing herself against the strong wind that blew up from the bay. The building itself had another large padlock. Trying several keys on the big chain Jim Duff had given her, she was successful on the fourth go. Sharon watched cormorants dive from a slip on one side. Ducks and seagulls congregated on the other side. She could even see fish – big ugly ones she couldn't identify.

Armed with binoculars, she climbed the twisty stairs to the top. The sky was streaked with pink and orange, in contrast to the deep mauve of the hills across the bay, and even more vibrant in the reflection on the water. From that height, Sharon could see swans in the basin ruffling their feathers, settling down for the night. On the beach, a dog ran after a stick and closer, people milled across the bridge that led into the medieval centre of the city. A few moments earlier, she'd seen the head of a seal dart up among the currents of the river after following fish in from the sea.

Sharon was aware of the importance of clean water. She had lectured women in rural Latin America to breast feed instead of mixing formula from dirty water. She tried to get them to stop washing clothes with strong soaps in the rivers. More importantly, she fought with communities to secure clean water supplies. This city was not in the third world. However, the water had been tested and judged unfit to drink. Sharon was hired to find out why.

The little tower was similar to a lighthouse with no light. Water was everywhere; on the bay where sailboats raced in the wind, in the rushing river and the quiet canals. Sharon felt as if she had finally found her spiritual home. She could never live far from water. She never failed to fall under its fascination. Perhaps that's why keeping the world's water clean had become both her job and a crusade. As a consultant she had been on every continent. It was a shame what man had done to his environment. Water was life.

She wondered where Jim Duff was, and if she would be able to spot him when he came out of the meeting. He'd seemed nicer today.

Little birds were lined up on an electricity line bobbing up and down in the wind. Others were flying in patterns in the sky. It was such a beautiful natural place with hardly any industry. Yet the irony was that even this place was spoiled.

Then she saw it. Coming out of a pipe near where she had seen the fish was a stream of brown liquid sludge. Mullet swarmed around the effluent. Ducks and other water birds swam up and huge river rats slinked down from the wall into the water for a feed. It wasn't the main source of contamination but at least it was one problem area identified. Tomorrow she would test the water. She'd now go back to the hotel and phone the councillor.

However, just then, a man in a city uniform came across the walkway, clicked the padlock into position and did the same at the gate. Oblivious to her banging on the window, he walked towards town.

As night fell, Sharon grew cold and miserable. She sat huddled on the floor, prepared for an uncomfortable stay. Desperate to go to the toilet, she averted her gaze from the windows and the sight of water all around. She tried thinking of the hot jungle she had hiked through in Latin America and started to name the birds and animals she had seen there to keep her mind off her predicament. Tapir. Sloth. Toucan ...

To pass time, she looked at fish hooks, nets and fisheries maps. Old record books tracked the salmon that swam upstream. Another monitored vessel movement. The river and canal was full of activity in the past centuries. There were mills, distilleries, stone-works and warehouses, all depending on the river for transport or energy.

A heron perched on the bank outside the tower, resting before its last bout of fishing for the day while there was still light.

Sharon thought of the old quote: 'Water, water everywhere and not a drop to drink.' She was determined she would make the water in this place good again. In most cases, water would make a recovery. There were exceptions: an arsenic leak from a gold mine or dioxins in a landfill site from illegal dumping of toxic waste. There was nothing drastic in this city though. She was sure she could make things better.

Suddenly she heard a noise downstairs. Someone was trying to open the lock. Sharon looked with trepidation at the door as it creaked open. Was it someone with sinister intent? Just in case, Sharon hid under an old canvas sail.

'If it's not a psycho,' thought Sharon. 'I'll hug whoever it is. I have to get out of here.'

Jim Duff had a look of concern as he walked through

the door. He was caught off guard when Sharon ran to him with her arms out.

"I called your hotel and they said you hadn't returned. I didn't think you were the type to be out partying all night."

"And why's that?"

"You strike me as much too responsible for that."

"I thought no one was coming."

He stroked her hair.

"Good news. We can afford you now." He told her the meeting he had with national politicians had resulted in more funds allocated to finding a solution to the water crisis.

Sharon smiled. "Absolutely delighted. But tell me back at the hotel. I have to rush to the toilet. By the way, I have some news for you. I found something. It is not the main problem, but it is a problem. "

"We don't want to lose you so soon."

"Don't worry," Sharon smiled. "I think I will be here for a while yet."

The lights from the city brightened and people strolled out to greet the night.

LIONS' DEN

Remy walked in the door dragging the baby llama by the hind legs so that the soft white neck swept the floor. Its face looked peaceful except for the dash of red behind the ear. The neck, though, was limp all the way down, a sure sign it was dead. Remy dropped the carcass and sat down on a stool.

"We're going to open him up in the morning. We'll take a knife, start at the end and slice up."

"Why?" was all I could manage.

"It had a disease." He took a cigarette, lit it and let it rest at the side of his mouth.

"It looked okay yesterday. It was running about," I said. "What was wrong?"

"We'll know tomorrow."

I wasn't going to give Remy the satisfaction of showing how I felt. When I first saw that llama, I thought it was one of the most beautiful creatures I had ever seen. Pure white – not a mark on him – with big black eyes and large teeth not yet stained by life. He was affectionate, rubbing against his mother, and it let me run my fingers through his soft wool before skipping away.

Remy threw the cigarette to the ground and stamped

it out. He reached behind his back and pulled out a large revolver that was tucked into his trousers.

"This is what we did it with."

"Did what?"

"Killed him."

It was a crude comment by a crude boy who had no respect for the beauty of life.

Remy fidgeted with the gun. It looked like it had a history. There was a long snout. It was tarnished, scratched and discoloured.

"This is Etienne's gun from Algeria!"

"What do you mean from Algeria?"

"From the war?"

"Etienne's too young to have fought in that war."

"Yes, but his father was there and gave him the gun. He really saw some action."

Remy wasn't actually pointing the gun at me but he was impulsive and I was getting nervous.

"Is the gun loaded?"

"What's the use of a gun that isn't loaded? Do you want to hold it?"

I put out my hands to take it. It was heavy and cold and, despite the disgust I felt, I wanted to fire it, to feel its warmth and power. Dropping it on the ground, I stepped back.

"Girls just don't know how to handle weapons. Etienne said I could keep it for a few days."

He picked up the gun and rubbed it as if he were cleaning it.

"I'm going out later to shoot at birds. Do you want to come?"

I shook my head. I looked down at the baby llama one last time and walked out.

"You won't be forgotten little one."

* * *

The animals were restless. The hyenas were at it all night. Wolves joined in, mixed with snorts and growls I did not recognize. Drifting into sleep, I saw the angelic face of the little llama dripping with blood.

At breakfast in the big old kitchen, everyone at the animal park was in a cheerful mood. The men had already eaten and gone. Marian was singing as she poured hot milk into the coffee cups. Charlotte was telling jokes. Ten years had been removed from her forehead. All lines had suddenly disappeared overnight.

"Monsieur is on a high. You can meet the baby today, perhaps look after her. Monsieur and I, we may ... " She broke off humming.

Both Marian and Charlotte checked me over to see if I was presentable. My hair had to be brushed again but they let everything else go. I followed Charlotte up the winding stairs and was surprised to find that they went nowhere in particular. Actually, they led to part of what used to be the upstairs of the castle that had been destroyed during a fire. An empty space remained after the debris having been cleared away. A door to the left gave on to a large room with stonewalls and floors, the only part of the upstairs to be salvaged. Bookcases lined three of the walls; an untidy desk and a double bed sat on either side of the room and right in

89

the middle stood a large old bathtub with golden feet. In it
was a man and what appeared to be a stuffed toy, both under
a high pile of bubbles. The man had attractive grey hair and
intense light blue eyes.

"This is the new au pair, notre petite Irlandaise,"
Charlotte announced. "And this is Monsieur Montourion."

The man clutched the teddy in one arm and stood up
in the bath with his other hand outstretched. I took his hand
and mumbled a hello, keeping my head slightly averted. But
in the end I couldn't help staring. The teddy was moving.

"This is the baby," Monsieur declared.

Still trying not to look at Monsieur, I could see this
little black face with small black eyes, a squashed nose and
a surprising crest of yellowish hair on top of the head.
Monsieur passed her to me. Her body felt warm and wet as it
lay in my arms. She looked up at me and extended one finger
as if making a rude sign. Then she put it up to my mouth.

"Go on," said Monsieur. "Suck her finger. That's how
she gives kisses. She likes you."

Her little black hands and feet were 'perfection'. There
were even tiny fingernails. I knew what a new mother must
feel like.

"A monkey!" I said at last.

"Mais no! Mountain gorilla, and quite rare with that
blonde hair on top. Charlotte and I were working on making
a little brother for her this very morning," Monsieur laughed.

He winked. Blood rushed to my cheeks and I felt hot
and uncomfortable. Charlotte pretended to be horrified
but her eyes were shining and she couldn't stop smiling.

She cupped her hands and scooped a large pile of bubbles and blew them at Monsieur. He grabbed and pulled her in the tub. They both came up out of the bubbles laughing. I walked over to the bed and put the gorilla down for a moment. She crawled on my shoulders, did somersaults, ran up and down and, to my delight, actually beat her chest like Tarzan.

There was another small room off this large one. Charlotte and Monsieur disappeared 'to get dry clothes on'. Charlotte came out alone after a while to show me where to find nappies, baby clothes and toys. I was told she ate mainly different types of cut up fruit.

"But only come up here if you have permission. If Monsieur is busy, he doesn't want to be bothered with people like us. You caught him on a good day today."

* * *

I was free to walk around the animal park in the afternoon when I had no *au pair* duties. Frightened to get attached after the llama episode, I still found myself picking out favourites. There was a black Russian wolf, one of the last of its kind that stared at me through green hungry eyes; the Siberian tiger with its luxurious and colourful coat; a tapir couple that always greeted me and ostriches that ran along side me or pecked my head from behind.

After weeks of rain, there was finally a day of sunshine. I started to go upstairs to do my duties with the baby gorilla, something I always looked forward to. Monsieur was sometimes there, but most of the time he was in the small

91

bedroom closed off to the side. Charlotte met me at the top of the stairs crying.

"I wouldn't go up there if I were you," she warned.

"But I have to get Rilla washed and fed."

"That will be taken care of," she sniffled.

"What's wrong Charlotte? What's wrong with your cheek," I asked.

"I may as well walk into the cage with the lions. I can't live with him." A tear dripped down her cheek emphasizing the nasty bruise.

"Wait, I'll come down with you," she said.

We sat down at the kitchen table and Marian served us cups of coffee.

Two women knocked at the door and walked in looking for Monsieur. Both were tall, slight, blonde and beautifully dressed.

"Who are you?" Charlotte asked rudely.

The one wearing the pink trouser suit answered.

"We're friends of Paul's from Paris. Models from when he was a fashion photographer, before ... well, we've kept in touch."

"And what are you doing here?"

It was now the turn of the girl in the short black skirt to answer.

"He phoned us and invited us down."

Charlotte's face twisted in anger.

"If you are his friends, you should know how sick he is. He is very bad today. You can't see him."

"He sounded fine on the phone," one said as they

both pressed towards the stairs, but Charlotte blocked them.

"How do you know where to go? Have you been here before?"

"At Christmas when you were at your mother's." The two women seemed to be teasing Charlotte, who began waving her arm and shouting.

"Get out, Get out!" she said.

They left with a shrug and a smirk.

We sat down again to our coffee and tried to comfort Charlotte when we heard a commotion outside. The two models were trying to get a ladder up to the roof. Charlotte ran out and tried to grab it.

"Whores, Paris whores," she screeched.

At that point everyone looked up. There on the roof stood Monsieur dressed in faded blue jeans and a white shirt. He looked down surveying everyone and everything. His arm was bent at the elbow and his hand slipped through an opening in his shirt like a perfect little Napoleon.

"Mind your own business, Charlotte," he shouted with authority. "They're coming up."

* * *

Sounds of partying came from the second floor well into the night. Charlotte's wailing mixed with the savage cries of the animals.

In the kitchen at breakfast, Charlotte sobbed silently. She looked up. One eye was shut and bruised. She didn't want to talk about it. There was no point in going upstairs so

I walked around the park for a long time and found myself talking to the animals.

When it began to rain, I went back to the chalet where I was staying. The bedroom was in a loft upstairs. Downstairs was a reception area and a little shop. There was never anyone in there because the zoo was closed for the season. I spent the day trying on sunglasses, looking at souvenirs and postcards. A younger Charlotte was in many of them. Charlotte and the Siberian tiger as a baby, Charlotte and a smaller version of the donkey and Charlotte giving the Asian bear a bottle. How beautiful she was! There was nothing sophisticated about her; she was just natural. At dinner I brought over a few postcards to talk to Charlotte about a time when everyone was young. But she burst into tears again.

Marian asked me back to her room to watch a film on television. We walked to the entrance, turned right at the barn, went around it and entered at the back. I hesitated a bit.

"Come on," said Marian.

I took a step forward.

"Isn't this the barn?" I asked.

"One of them, yeah. But I live upstairs," she replied.

There were three rooms. The end one was Remy's. He lived over the boars, wart hogs and other wild pigs. Marian lived in the middle room over the hippos. The bedroom over the lions was empty.

"The floor is really rotten. I wouldn't like to live there," she said.

Marian had done up her room cosily. There was a frilly bedspread on the double bed, a little table with ornaments on it and a television in the corner. There were no smells or sounds from the occupants below – the hippos. Marian got me a chair and threw on some cushions. She turned on the TV. There was a cowboy film starting. And although it was hard for me to understand, I enjoyed being with people for a change.

Marian told me that she had a boyfriend who lived with her but that I had to promise never to mention anything to Monsieur. Not long afterwards there was a knock and there he was. Marian was about three times his size but Patrice made her feel like a starlet. He put his arm around her middle and hugged.

"Patrice is from Algeria," Marian said.

"Oh, was he in Algeria with Etienne's father?" I asked.

"No, Patrice is *from* there. Etienne's father was just there during the war." The couple looked uncomfortable.

We turned back our attention to the film and became so enthralled that when a knock came to the door, we all jumped. It was Remy.

"I got six birds with that gun!" he whispered.

"I don't want to know," I whispered back.

He offered to give me a bird but I told him I didn't want to hear about killing animals again. When he tried to take my hand to mirror the couple on the bed, I pulled it away.

However, I let Remy walk me back to my chalet. There were no outdoor lights and I didn't want to walk in with the hyenas. Remy tried to kiss me at the door but I pushed him away.

I slept so soundly that I did not notice the sun had risen and that the animals were in full chorus. When I looked out the window, I saw Monsieur walking quickly towards the chalet wearing knee-high leather boots. He stormed in and slammed the door.

"Come down here," he shouted.

I was still wearing my nightgown but went down anyway. He pointed to the racks of postcards and the stands of sunglasses.

"Did you touch those?" he asked.

"Yes, I did," I admitted. "They are lovely."

"Did you take any?"

"No, of course not. I was looking through the postcards to learn more about the place and what the animals were like as babies. The sunglasses? I tried them on one day I was bored. I never know what to do here. I haven't looked after the Rilla for a while."

It was as if he hadn't heard me. He started screeching.

"No wonder we don't make any money here. You pack your things."

I thought I was being fired as an au pair but what he had in mind was, in a way, far worse. When I had dressed and packed, he told me to follow him. We walked around the barn and up the stairs to where Marian lived. But we didn't go to visit Marian. He put my bags down in front of the first door. He took out a key, unlocked the door and opened it wide.

"Voila! Your new room," he said.

I looked around. The walls were covered in stained

peeling flowered wallpaper. Cobwebs hung down in the corners. The floor by the window was partly eaten away.

"But there are lions below."

"Get used to it," he said

I didn't go down to lunch. I put the clean sheets that Marian had given me on the narrow lumpy cot, crawled under the covers and cried to the sounds of lions. Later I got up and walked into the village. I just kept going. A car stopped and a young man told me to jump in. He was going to a dance in Normandy and asked me to go with him.

It was a long drive, but when we finally got to the sea, we played in the sand, waded in the cool Atlantic and ate mussels in a little café overlooking the beach. After that there was a dance, the reason he had come. It was a bit old-fashioned. The girls danced by themselves while the men smoked, drank and circled. Sometimes a boy would dance with a girl but he usually rushed away quickly after it was finished. There were fights going on outside and they didn't want to miss them.

I fell asleep on the way back to my new room, a bit more content now. The dance was almost as crazy as life with the animals.

* * *

When I went down for breakfast, I thought I saw Charlotte trying to hide a smile. I didn't feel very well. I had the flu. Marian heated up a liquid and told me to drink it down and go to bed.

"It's hot Cointreau," she said. "That will fix you up."

I went in and out of dreams. I didn't know where I was. When I woke up, Marian was in the room bringing in a tray.

"Well, sleepy head, how do you feel?" she asked.

My limbs no longer ached, I didn't have a headache, my fever had gone, and my head and nose were clear.

"Much better," I said.

"I should hope so."

"What do you mean?"

"You have been out for four days."

I got a lift into town and bought some white paint and a paintbrush. Remy volunteered to help me decorate my room. We put a dressing table to divide the part that was safe to walk on from the part that wasn't. We had the three walls painted in no time but the one near the window was almost impossible without a long pole. Once I forgot about the rotten floorboards and almost fell through. Remy caught me just in time or I would have been a lion's dinner.

Later I watched the African storks with their long beaks and exotic black and white feathers. Across the road there was a wooded area surrounding some fields. Bored, I thought I would explore while there was warmth in the sun. I went deeper and deeper into the woods. A cuckoo cried out.

The woods opened up into a meadow. A large rusty oil drum, with holes cut out for doors and windows, stood in the middle. An old man was sitting on a stump outside.

"You're the foreigner. I've heard about you." He looked close into my face with squinted eyes. I sat down.

"I suppose I am," I said. "But some people say that

Marian is a foreigner although she was born here and doesn't speak Polish. And Patrice, I'm not sure about. I think he is from Algeria but he says he is French."

"Yes, that was a bad business we had in Algeria," he snorted.

My mouth opened. "You were there?"

"I will never get over it. It wasn't even what we did to those people. There were others. I remember a bunch of Spaniards, Communists. They had escaped from Franco to the south of France, down to Morocco and over to Algeria. Well ... the leader's back in Spain now. I've seen him on the television. He doesn't walk right. Of course we were under orders. All that's over now."

He looked around as if frightened there was someone watching him too closely.

"So, you're at the zoo?"

"Yes," I said. "I suppose all the animals can be called foreigners too."

"They're not as weird as some of the people there."

"I've noticed," I replied.

He pointed his hands to his chest. "And they think I'm strange! They call me 'the drunk'. I have a little red wine once in a while to warm up the blood. Just because I live out here ... "

"It must be cold here in the winter," I said trying to change the subject a bit as he was getting excited.

His hands came together and he started rubbing them.

"It's not so bad. Etienne brings me what I need. Food. Warmth. If it is really bad out, there is a shed at the zoo. I want what everyone else wants: love, power, an understanding of the Universe. When I look up at the stars on a black night, I think I have been given the whole lot."

I felt small compared to this man. He later told me his name was Henri.

"You watch yourself there," he warned. "It's not the animals that will destroy themselves." He shook his head.

* * *

All the clothes I had bought in Paris were getting too tight. Because of boredom and the good French food, I was eating too much. I was not a stranger to an idle life in closed spaces. As a teenager I made a little room out of my closet and used to read and drink tea there. I didn't expect to do the same in France. I was alone most of the time, talking to animals, looking into the eyes of the tiger and the wolf one after each other, feeling caged like them, pulled down to earth rather than soaring with the stars. I poured my heart out to a little donkey that stared ahead of itself and then suddenly began braying for no apparent reason.

Reading had kept me up for several nights. I had picked up a book called *Watership Down*, a story about a journey by rabbits. It was so good I thought I would skip dinner, but went down to the kitchen at the last moment. There was the usual starter of charcuterie followed by soup, a delicious stew and a Cointreau and *chantilly* cream crepe for dessert. I lingered after dinner longer than usual as a good mood seemed to have returned to everyone.

"Just look at that moon," said Marian as light poured

100

in the window. We stared without saying anything. To keep the conversation going, I complimented Marian on her dinner.

"It's good, the rabbit stew," she commented.

"Rabbit?"

"Yes, it's very ... "

I didn't hear her last sentence. I just ran back to my room, getting sick on the lawn. It was weeks before I picked up the *Watership Down* book again.

That night I awoke again not knowing where I was. Moonlight was streaming into the room. There were no curtains. The animals were making more noise than usual. Careful not to walk on any rotten floorboards, I went over to the window and looked out. Floating around the park was a white goddess with long flowing hair, a billowing delicate cloth wrapped around her. Some clouds passed over the moon and disappeared. She looked like some strong and beautiful angel. I watched her for a long time. Then she turned the corner near the shed.

Sleep was impossible. I wondered if I was hallucinating. I threw back the covers and went over to the kitchen for coffee. There was no one there. Everyone was out in the yard or bustling round the sheds. Etienne seemed to have brought some friends to help. Some of the animals had escaped, the doors of their cages left open wide. The tiger was the most serious fugitive but the situation wasn't as bad as it could have been. He had been de-clawed and was used to people as he was raised at the zoo since he was a cub. Monkeys hung off workers' shoulders and various types of pigs were running in all directions. The parrot was squawking. Marian, Charlotte, Remy and Patrice were all helping herd animals back to their homes.

Later everyone lounged around and waited for the coffee that Marian had gone off to get.

"God-damn," said Etienne, kicking the truck.

He circled the vehicle and swore at each end. The tyres had been slashed. Then he checked the tractors and all the cars. The same thing. He threw his hat down on the ground, stamped it into the earth and swore again.

"She was here last night," said Charlotte.

"Who?" I asked.

"Monsieur Montourion's crazy whore of an ex-wife, Lise, from Paris," said Charlotte. "From the asylum. She's escaped again. Did you see anything?"

"I thought I saw a lady with long hair dressed in long flowing robes," I said, not ready to let go of her, wanting to keep the mysterious woman to myself.

"That's her. She wants to destroy us. They should throw away the key."

Later I asked Marian about the woman. She said Lise, a model, had had a break-down when Monsieur was a fashion photographer in Paris. The doctors told him it was unlikely she would recover. However, he had refused to divorce her and therefore couldn't marry Charlotte. A sore point.

Devastated about his wife's condition, Monsieur had quit his job to become a wildlife photographer in Africa for the Association for the Prevention of Cruelty to Gorillas. Many gorillas were being slaughtered for their land, for meat, for the pleasure of it.

"They kill the closest animal to man," said Marian. "Savages all of them."

"Why didn't he stay in Africa?" I ask.

"Look at the pictures sometimes. Bleeding bodies, hands cut off, skinned carcasses, mass slaughter. He thought if he could get some of them out of there, he would be doing good. Then he started the zoo to help pay for it all."

I thought back to the postcards I had looked through in the office. The castle untouched by fire. Monsieur good-looking and happy. Charlotte young and cheerful. What had happened to change everything so much?

"It must have been hard with the fire."

I had always been reluctant to bring up the subject of the charred remains of most of the castle.

Marian sighed.

"Everyone knows it was Lise who started it but there's no proof. Charlotte was at her mother's. Monsieur was lucky enough to get out but several of the apes were lost. It took a great deal out of us all."

* * *

Braying came from over the wall. I peeked over and saw Etienne exercising the baby donkey. They both saw me. Etienne had never spoken to me before and I felt a bit timid. He was so strong and self-assured but gentle at the same time. He had a real gift in handling animals. They seemed to trust him. He treated me the same way as he did the animals.

"Come," he said.

I followed like a little puppy. He took my hand and

pushed it on to the donkey's head and stroked it, his hand over mine. He made a sign with his head for me to continue stroking the animal. There was a piece of rope around the donkey's neck. He pulled gently on it and the donkey followed. We walked across the road to enter the forest. I looked back and saw Remy standing there with a cigarette out the side of his mouth glaring at us. The donkey liked the woods and we had to pull on the rope or it would have raced though them. Even keeping him to a fast walk, we had to run to keep up. We were soon in the field.

"Hello Papa."

I hadn't known that Etienne was Henri's son.

"You gave me a fright. I didn't expect that beast."

He put his hands on the donkey's flanks and took a look at the teeth.

"He's a fine one."

"The first one born over there. It wasn't that easy."

"Ah, he'll be grand."

"You take him back," Etienne said to me. "I want to sit here a while with Henri. We have some things to talk about."

Charlotte met me at the entrance.

"You have got to hide. Quick."

She passed the donkey to Remy and indicated for me to follow her. We crept silently hiding behind whatever gave us shelter. We made a run for it from behind the big wheels of the tractor to the door of the Asian bears' den.

"What's wrong?" I asked.

"Shh! That Paris bastard has followed you here. Remember the one on the Metro you gave your address here to so that you could get rid of him then. Stupid thing to do! I'm sure he is the one. Anyway, he's asking for you. I said you weren't here."

'I never thought he'd actually come all the way up here," I murmured.

Charlotte beckoned to Remy who was coming out of the shed.

"Take her and hide her in with the pigs. No one will find her there."

The smell preceded them. I had seen the small ones roaming around, the *pecaris* from South America. The big ones, wild boars and wart hogs, had been enclosed in a pen that led to a barn where they slept at night. It was pitch black so we had to feel along the walls to know where we were going. Remy gripped my shoulders.

"Stay here. Get down, squat."

I could see the end of his rolled-up cigarette smouldering.

"I'll be back to get you when it's all clear. If you don't move, you won't have a problem."

I tried to be still and silent. Although it was totally dark, the image of sharp yellowing tusks was clear in my mind. Rough back bristles brushed against my leg. At times I even felt that Remy was watching me. The worst were the sounds: the snorts, the nuzzling in hay, the short, hot breaths.

There are stories of ordinary farmyard pigs falling on a person and eating them all up. I started to imagine myself not being able to stay still anymore, being set upon by these fierce filthy things. I could feel hot breath on my cheek and was ready to risk running out when Remy came in and told me the man had gone.

Remy walked me to my room where I got toiletry supplies and rushed to the shower. Even there I imagined eyes upon me and hurried. Scrub out that pig smell and everything will be fine I told myself. I left my dirty clothes in the shower and put on a clean nightgown. Although it was still light out, I crawled into bed. A knock on the door made me jump.

"It's Remy. Let me in. I want to see that you are ok."

"I'm fine Remy. Just tired. I'm going to go to bed," I replied.

"Well, open the door a minute to say good night."

"Okay Remy. Just a moment."

He walked by me and sat at a chair near the bed. "You did all right in there. Most girls would have been scared."

"I was scared," I said.

He got up and came over to me.

"Give me a kiss." I looked at him with exhaustion.

"No Remy, I will not kiss you."

"Why not?" he asked.

"I am much too old for you."

"I'm a man. I'm mature for eighteen."

"I know you are. But it's not going to happen."

He started rolling up his sleeves. Flinching, I thought he was going to hit me but he held out his arms. They were covered in raw sores.

"Remy, what happened to you?" I felt sympathetic yet disgusted at the same time. I instinctively moved away. He took another puff on his cigarette. Then he held out his arm and put the lit end onto his skin.

"I love you," he said.

"No, you don't love me. Now leave me alone. You are mad," I yelled. After he slunk out of the door, my self-control dropped and I cried myself to sleep.

* * *

Remy and I avoided each other after that. Whenever I saw him, he just scowled at me. Sometimes he took out that horrid gun and started to play with it. I couldn't bear another empty weekend so I planned to visit the north of France. Not bothering to tell anyone, I got a lift to town to catch a train to Lille. With each click of the wheels, I relaxed more. However, I was on the last of my money. I had already been at the zoo for three months and had not been paid anything. Not that I had been doing much to get paid for. But I was willing. I would have to sort that out when I got back.

There was an English woman I knew living in Lille. I hoped she was there. The only telephone at the zoo was in Monsieur Montourion's office so I hadn't been able to call in advance.

I looked out the window of the train as a tourist. Behind me were the lions, the pigs and the apes. Left back there was a young man with a twisted sense of love.

The train pulled into Lille. It was good to be in a big city again. Movement. Car noise. Life. A bus from the station left me a few blocks from Elizabeth's apartment. An old woman let me enter the building as she went in. It was a long climb to the top floor apartment. There was no one home. After leaving a note, I went to read in a small café squeezed between local shops. Every so often I phoned but there was never any answer. Money was a problem. I just had enough to get a *pension* for the night. Then I'd have to go back to the zoo with my return ticket without a cheery English voice to raise my spirits!

My stomach knotted as I saw the burnt tower again. It was silent and shuttered and with each step, I felt impending dread. I ran up the stairs of the barn to my room and bolted the door. Someone had been in there. My bed covers were tousled. On my bedside table was a page torn out of a copybook. I picked it up. On the page were lines in childish printing with bad grammar and misspellings. There was no name on it but I knew it was from Remy. It went something like this:

"I will kill any animal for you. All for you."

His small eyes, the jutting-out chin, the gold tooth, the burns on his arm came into focus. I shuddered.

* * *

"You were supposed to be selling tickets at the entrance, and then working in the creperie. The zoo is now open."

"I didn't know. Wasn't I hired to look after Rilla?"

He looked down at his feet.

"That didn't work out. Don't look at me like that. You owe me. I've fed you well and given you a place to sleep.

"Like the animals in the cages," I mumbled.

"What did you say?"

108

"Nothing."

I looked over at Rilla who made little noises to me and put out her little black finger for me to kiss. Realizing I had been taken on as cheap labour, I felt cheated.

The only visitors to the entrance booth that afternoon were the pair of tapirs who started rubbing each other next to me.

The creperie was empty but Etienne and Patrice pretended to be customers so I could practice my waitressing skills. By the end I could manage a tray with one hand without everything falling off. I remembered the names of all the crepes and the drinks to go with them.

On the way back to the entrance booth, I saw Etienne and Remy go into the shed with machetes. Etienne gave me a smouldering look and I thought for a moment that he too was angry with me. Then he turned around and winked. Remy beckoned to me but I signalled that I was late. He insistently pointed into the shed, and being curious, I reached there just in time to see a machete slash through the carcass of the baby donkey. Remy drew his hand across his neck as I looked in horror.

"Disease," said Etienne shaking his head.

I ran to the ticket booth at the entrance, trying to keep the tears back. Pain and death seemed to be everywhere. Seven o'clock closing time came without a single customer. I would have preferred to roam rather than being trapped in a box for hours on end doing nothing. I skipped dinner. Besides feeling sick by the sight of the donkey, I was determined to pull myself together. If I didn't do anything, I would soon be as big as Marian who pretended that she was big-boned. I know it bothered her the way they secretly looked down on her because of her weight, and because she was 'a foreigner', a foreigner like me.

My room was macabre; something was upsetting the lions underneath. Counting out the money in my purse, I decided I could afford one night out.

I walked down the hill to the café, picking *coquecots* or small poppies as I went. Several old men stood at the counter of the bar and stared as I walked in.

"A bottle of red wine, please." I said.

"Right away, Mademoiselle," answered the man, also old, behind the counter.

"There you go. A bottle of red. And this is for your flowers."

He placed the bottle and a wine glass in front of me; then took the flowers and put them in a soft drink bottle filled with water. I picked up the wine bottle and offered it to the nearest of the old men. When all their glasses were full, they looked around uncomfortably as if waiting for something. Then one of them gestured to the poppies, holding his glass out proudly.

"To the war," he said.

"To the war," said the others.

"To Mademoiselle," said another.

"To Mademoiselle," followed the others.

Later I asked them what war they were referring to and each one seemed to be talking about a different one.

Etienne and Remy had slipped in and were sitting at a

table in the back near the entrance. They were drinking beer. The old men saw them but did not speak or acknowledge them in any way. The wine was going to my head and the horror of the donkey was coming back to me. I slipped off the stool. I had to get out of there and I headed to the door.

"Don't forget your flowers," the bar man called after me.

But poppies were not going to change anything.

Etienne whispered to me on his way out.

"We don't tell stories about the castle to outsiders."

"I'm not telling stories," I said. "I don't know any. I don't understand anything here."

"It's dark. I'd better walk you home."

Still angry with him about the donkey I snorted that I was quite capable of going home myself. Remy scowled in the corner.

"What's going to attack me?" I asked. "A wild animal? Sure they're my house-mates.'

I was a bit wobbly going up the hill and thought it would have been nice to have Etienne to lean on. Someone strong. The moon hung heavy and yellow over the blackened ruins of the castle.

Worried about the hole in the floor, I felt carefully for the bed as the light switch wasn't working. Marian came in with an oil lamp.

"Power's off everywhere. Probably Madame again. This will get you through 'til the morning but be careful. With this dry wood, the barn could go up in minutes."

"I'll be careful," I assured her.

"You ok?" she asked.

"I'm fine. Just a bit tired."

"Well, bolt your door just in case. You never know where Madame will go."

I had no more interest in the white lady. What was I thinking? A symbol of hope? She was nothing but a mad woman. The lock was rusty and I struggled to slide it over. I put the matches beside my bed and blew out the flame of the lamp. My eyes adjusted to moonlight and I could make out shapes in the room before falling asleep.

In my dream I became the white lady and I was dancing with Henri around the fields near his oil drum. We were free and happy and light. We were spirit. Then it changed. Animals were devouring one another. Stop! Stop! Stop! I sat up in my bed awake. There was banging on my door.

"Let me in." It was Remy.

"Go away," I said.

"Let me in."

"I was asleep. Go away."

Pounding again. "I just want one kiss. I love you."

"You'll wake up Patrice and Marian."

"If you let me in, I won't make any more noise."

"I'm not going to let you in Remy. It is late. Go to bed"

It sounded as if he was trying to knock the door down with his shoulder.

"You've had too much to drink Remy. Go to bed and we'll talk about it tomorrow."

He seemed to be crying.

"No, I've waited long enough. I want to kiss you. I want to make love to you."

"No."

"I have Etienne's gun. I'll kill myself if you don't let me in."

"Don't be foolish, Remy."

"I'll do it. The Algerian gun you like so much. I'll shoot myself right in the heart with it. If you don't let me in, I won't be able to stand the pain."

I don't think I've ever heard a shot that close before. I had gone partridge hunting with my uncles but the shot didn't sound as loud and as clear as the one on the other side of my door. I heard nothing from Remy except a weight falling to the floor. By that time Marian and Patrice were up. Marian kept screaming, which was out of character for her. She told me to stay in my room until she got Monsieur Montourion. Moonlight lit up the door. Everyone was now on the other side. I could hear Monsieur Montourion and the ambulance attendants talking. Then people moved away. Marian offered to stay with me that night. A doctor came later and gave me a shot.

During the night, I woke up screaming.

"It's not your fault. You didn't do anything." Marian said.

"I killed him," I screeched. "I killed him."

"But he's not dead." said Marian quietly. "He missed his heart by an inch."

The sight of the gun and the blood outside of my room drove me into hysterics again. Patrice came out of Marian's room.

"We can't move anything until the police say we can."

He and Marian whispered to each other for a minute.

"Don't feel bad. It's not your fault," he said. "Come on, I want to show you something."

I walked down the corridor, both of them on either side of me. We passed the door to their room and came to Remy's. Patrice opened the door.

"We wanted to spare you but I think you should look. He was crazy."

Inside, one wall was completely papered in naked pinup girls with hearts drawn in blue ink and my name over them.

* * *

When I came to, I was in the loft over the gatehouse office. I didn't feel bad anymore but it was time to say goodbye. A postal order had come from my mother so I had enough money to get to Paris and fly home. My ticket was safely hidden inside my French grammar book. There were still a few days to wait and I wanted to keep busy, to work in the creperie or even the reception but no one would let me.

"Rest," they said.

On the day I was to leave I went down to the oil drum for the last time, passing Etienne. He smiled at me in his controlled mysterious way.

"Henri," I said. "I've decided to go home, flawless French or not. There are other things I've learned."

He covered my hands with his.

"There is always material to learn from when we are ready."

"You are so wise, Henri, I will miss you."

"I am neither the good man or the bad man," he replied.

Pulling my hands gently away, I was emotional.

"Au revoir," I whispered.

Henri, not showing that he knew what had happened over the past few days, only grunted. In spite of his wildness, Henri had always been such a formal, intelligent man. But he pursed his lips and started uttering monkey sounds. I laughed as he began jumping up and down, swinging me around. He went through a range of noises reproduced with precision after years of exposure. There was the *ou ou ou* of Rilla, the crude laugh of the hyenas, the squealing in different ranges of the various pigs (sharp and high for the *pecaris* and low for the wart hogs), the *aowuowuowu* howl of the lone Russian wolf, the deep roar of the tiger; a whole concerto of my stay there. The animals across the road answered back.

Charlotte had my suitcases in the car. She gave me the postcard of her feeding the baby Asian bears and looking so young.

"Monsieur won't be down," she said. "He's in one of his moods. Rilla says goodbye though."

For the first time Charlotte looked at me with a sort of respect, even envy.

"I have to leave here too someday. I'm going to leave, I swear, or I'll walk right in the lion's cage and let them feed on my bones."

The gates closed and the car started to coast down the hill towards the village. I didn't look back but I watched as Charlotte glanced over her shoulder and we both gave a slight shiver knowing that even with the strongest intentions, she would never leave.

BEACHED IN DUBLIN

Everybody told me it wasn't right to live with my in-laws, especially with the baby coming. I had heard all the mother-in-law jokes and read column after column of advice on that topic. Yet I remained unconvinced.

When I arrived in Dublin in the eighties, it was a depressing place. Young people were leaving in order to find work and many of those left behind were without hope. Donal and I got married in New York, where I was living. But now that there was a baby on the way, Donal wanted to move back to Ireland. I was quite happy to escape the hectic pace for a new life with my new husband and little January, our unborn child.

We moved in with Donal's parents in a quiet residential area in Dublin. I was happy there but something kept nagging me to move. After three months, I felt we should be getting our own place. I didn't want to impose on his parents any longer and felt it would be better to be on our own.

It was difficult to adapt to some things. I had always been used to working. When I applied for waitressing jobs, one look at my bulging front, prospective employers just shook their heads. Some said the eighties were just a bad time in Ireland.

'Not much work here even for our own, Love," they said.

Donal got a job right away. In fact, he had so many hours in overtime that I often found myself alone and was beginning to feel a bit down. It was Mrs. Fray, Donal's mother, who comforted me. I would sit down in the sunroom overlooking the garden, still colourful in winter, and she would bring me hot chocolate. Mrs. Fray, or Bláthnaid, was easy to get on with and I felt she was more of a friend than a mother-in-law.

Donal agreed that we should rent our own little flat, but after looking at a few near the city centre, I found everything small or dirty. Each flat turned out to be worse and I knew I would find it hard to leave the comfort and pampering at the Fray house.

With the newspaper spread out on the table in front of me in the breakfast nook, I sipped my coffee.

"You're going out again then?"

Mr. Fray tapped his pipe against the ashtray.

"Yes, I'll just have a peek at one place, stay in town for lunch and then meet Donal back at the flat so he can check it out too. I don't know. I'm terribly discouraged."

He yawned. "Well, if that's what you want, I'm sure you'll find something. Now, do you know the way?"

I had it memorized, the 46A to Trinity and then the 15 to South Circular Road, or I could walk. Depending on how I felt. Depending on the weather.

Mr. Fray offered to take me as far as the bus. A light drizzle surrounded me at the bus stop. I pulled my coat tighter but it wouldn't close over the bump, now very large. The bus driver was impatient when I struggled to get up the stairs. I ignored him, paid the right amount, and continued up the windy steps to the upper level. I always enjoyed looking over the walls into people's front gardens from the top of a double-decker bus.

The flat I was viewing that afternoon was down a quiet cul-de-sac, a twenty-minute walk from the city centre. It was a small cottage with an unkempt front garden and a worn path to the door. The neighbours seemed to keep their gardens tidy and colourful and, with a little work, I was sure our garden could bloom too. Number ten. I got the key from the neighbour and struggled with the stuck door before it flung open.

First impressions were not good. The sofa and chairs tried to look elegant in antique gold plush but failed miserably because of dodgy looking stains and holes from cigarettes. I told myself that it wasn't that bad. They could be covered with one of those bright cotton Indian blankets.

The walls were filthy and would have to be painted. Donal would have to do it. I couldn't stand the fumes. Something neutral would do. A soft grey perhaps.

The kitchen was small but I didn't plan to spend much time in it. There were loads of dishes in the cupboards. The table and chairs in the corner were of good wood. I checked the oven and burners. All fine. But as I pulled out the tray under the grill, a stench of rancid grease hit me. My stomach jolted. I walked over to the window, opened it and took in deep breaths.

I should be careful. What if I needed to reach Donal in an emergency? There was no phone here and I didn't have a mobile. My hand strayed on to my belly as I felt a kick.

"Anything for independence," I thought to myself calming down. "It's small but, fixed up, we could have our own little family alone together."

I walked into one of the bedrooms. The bed would have to be taken out and a cot put in. It would have to be painted too.

The bathroom was a shock. It was dark; there were no windows. It was painted a bright pink and there were mushrooms growing out of the pipe into the toilet.

The other bedroom was not much bigger than the other one. My hand reached out to feel the double bed, which took up most of the space in the room. I should at least try it. I sank into the middle of the bed where it sagged. I tried to roll off but was awkward and clumsy so I couldn't quite manage it. Like a beetle stuck on its back, I wiggled my legs and arms in the air. There was no escape.

I patted my belly gently and began to sing a lullaby. "Don't worry, little one. We'll be okay."

When Donal came into the flat an hour later, he found me wedged down in the mattress, tears dripping down my face.

"We'll need a new bed," I said.

Donal sat on the edge as I told him of the dirty upholstery, the filthy walls, the sickening grease and the mushrooms in the bathroom.

"But, the beds are the worst. I think they are dirty. At

the very least, they are uncomfortable. We can't bring a baby into this."

Donal hugged me and helped me up. I half-laughed through the tears when he said I looked like a beached whale.

We left the keys into the neighbour's and I waddled behind Donal to the bus stop. However, we wouldn't have to take the bus home. Mr. Fray was waiting in the car for us. Donal had phoned him before he called in at the flat and he had offered to pick us up.

"We thought we'd lost you," he said. "There's no rush you know. You can stay with us as long as you like."

I cuddled next to Donal in the back seat and patted my tummy. There was nothing wrong with being comfortable I decided. Perhaps we should just stay where we were until something nicer came up.

GIFTED

Jack was seated at a table by himself at Taylor's Pub with a pint of Guinness in front of him when his younger brother came through the door and walked over to him excitedly. Tom stood in front of Jack with a big smile on his face. He sat down and pounded the table causing yellowish foam to slide down Jack's glass.

"I did it Jack," he said, "I quit my job. I'm free now to write full time."

Jack was delighted for him. He knew the teaching job was like a yoke around his brother's neck. He could still hear his mother's voice, God rest her soul, telling Tom never to give up a secure, pensionable job, always reminding him of the sacrifices they had made to give him an education, something Jack had to forego in order to start working. Jack could never understand Tom's unrest. A job was a job, but if he was happy to be finished with it, then Jack was happy for him.

"That's great Tom," he said, "What are you having? Pint of Guinness?"

Lost in his own thoughts, Tom nodded his head. When Jack came back with the pint, he took a big sip and put the glass down on the table.

"Don't worry about my part of the rent," he assured Jack. "I get paid all summer and I can get the dole after that."

Jack held up his pint glass in a toast.

"I'm not worried," he said.

"I've given myself a year to be able to earn a living by writing," said Tom.

"Here's to you then," Jack nodded.

The two brothers had always been close. They were both in their late thirties, a three-year age difference. Jack had left school early to join his father in the forge while Tom had gone on to be a teacher. Neither had married as their mother had been ill. They had lived in the family home until their mother's death but the house had to be sold to pay off debts. Although each brother lived different lives, it seemed natural that they get an apartment together.

Now that Tom was no longer working, a new routine was soon established. Jack and Tom woke up at seven in the morning and had breakfast together. Jack went off to the forge where he worked on kitchen chairs, gate railings and a line of candlesticks. He was happy that the job had turned more creative, although he had enjoyed making tools. Tom sat down at the computer to write his masterpiece. An hour later he would be still staring at a blank screen. Early days. It would come. He just needed inspiration.

Sports were a great source of enjoyment for Jack. Not only did he watch it as a spectator, he still actually played soccer. Because he had excelled in rowing in secondary school, he coached young people twice a week after work. The fresh air made him feel alive as he moved the small motorboat through the swans and the ducks, calling out instructions to the young team.

Tom usually waited for Jack to come home for dinner. It was not so much that he didn't know how to cook but since Jack did the shopping, he seemed to have some sort of plan and it was easier just to leave everything to him. Tired of sitting alone in front of the computer all day, Tom sought out the company of his friends in a trendy café for a few hours after they finished work. Dressed in black with a beret and a leather jacket, he fit right in with the discussions about films and books. And even though most of his friends were teachers, there was an artistic aura around them.

At home, Jack had cleared up the breakfast and lunch dishes before preparing the dinner. Tom got home just as he was setting the table.

"How's the writer?" he asked.

"Fine," said Tom. "I'm starving."

After dinner, they both settled down to watch a bit of television. Once the programme ended, Tom stretched and got up.

"Don't wait up. I'm going to that new film and might have a pint after that."

Jack turned off the television, did the washing, poured himself a whiskey and sat down at the computer.

The next day Tom came home with an antique Olivetti typewriter, thinking it would inspire him to start writing. He practised pressing down the keys and loved the sound they made. However, another day went by without Tom writing anything coherent. Rather than stare at the new machine, he went out to meet his friends.

Tom's dinner was left in the warming oven. After clearing up, Jack sat down at the computer. Every so often he got up and put another piece of turf on the fire. Tom stumbled home late after a night at the pub and went straight upstairs to bed. Jack paused until he was certain Tom had got up the stairs all right, and then he went back to typing at the computer. Tom could hear the tapping at the keyboard from upstairs and covered his ears with his pillow.

Staying in bed the next day, Tom stumbled down the stairs to find Jack standing at the cooker, whistling a traditional tune.

"I don't feel so well today. I'll just have a bite to eat and go upstairs again," he said.

He helped himself to a chip from the pan and dropped it quickly as it burned his fingers. They ate dinner in silence. Then Tom sat back.

"You must be tired yourself, Jack. I heard you on the computer all night. What were you doing?"

Jack shrugged.

"Just messing," he said.

When Tom asked him how long he had been doing that, Jack said he had done it since they got the PC.

It was a good summer for once. Streets were filled with people strolling, sitting in the hastily organised outdoor cafes or restaurants, or lying on the grass in the city parks.

Tom was determined to keep at the writing and would sit for hours in front of the typewriter. Yet he continued to get a blank stare from the white paper. He went into town and bought a fancy notebook and a good pen. Still nothing.

What made it worse was that Jack wrote on the computer every night. Tom, home from the pub, would go up to his bedroom and put the pillow over his head. He had almost stopped talking to his brother and had become sullen and lethargic.

When Jack was at work one day, Tom searched the files on the computer to find out what his brother had been writing. He eventually opened a file called 'In the Forge' to find a large series of poems.

"Not half bad," he said to himself.

Tom joined Jack for dinner that night instead of taking his plate up to his room as had been his habit for the past few weeks. He even helped Jack with the dishes. As he was putting away the dishcloth, he turned to his brother.

"I didn't know you wrote poetry," he said.

Jack again shrugged it off. "I'm just messing," he said.

Something in Jack's calm manner, his facile attitude to his poems caused Tom to let out all his own frustrations. He moved closer to Jack and looked straight into his face.

"I thought I was the writer in this family." He clenched his fists. "I gave up my job for it," he said.

Jack didn't move.

"There is no argument. You are the writer," he said.

Tom frowned. "But I can't write anything with you banging away."

Jack shrugged. "I'll stop so. No problem," he said. "It'll come to you soon." and he walked up to his room.

The confrontation did nothing to solve Tom's writer's block though. He sat at his desk day after day until he got fed up and went out.

The two brothers had been eating separately and kept to their rooms when they were at home. There was still no movement on Tom's novel. Feeling guilty for attacking his brother, Tom knocked on his door to apologise. When Jack said to enter, Tom opened the door and saw him lying on the bed writing longhand into a notebook. Tom felt his face burn and every nerve in his body tense. He grabbed an oar standing against the doorframe that Jack had brought home to varnish for the rowing team he coached.

"I told you Jack," Tom shouted as he hit him repeatedly over the head with the oar. "I -am -the -writ -er -in -the -family."

Each syllable was emphasised by a crack on the head. "I -am -the -writ -er."

Crimson spread through Jack's black hair. He went limp and then was still. Tom dropped the oar and went over and lifted his brother's head. The notebook which had fallen onto the bed, was open to the page Jack was writing on. It said: coffee, eggs, washing up liquid, sausages, veget ...

THE RIGHT MOVES

It was on one of those walks by the wild river that Margaret developed her plan. She didn't know if she'd be brave enough to carry it through but it was nice to have it there in her head. Having done the shopping, she went to a little accessory shop on her way home and picked out a stick-on belly button jewel, the deep blue one to go with her eyes.

One child home from school. Homework. Music practice. Second child home. Homework. Extra spelling practice. Go out to play. In and out while she made dinner. It was special tonight. Steamed clams. A little garlic, onion and parsley, a splash of wine, the lid put on firmly. Serve with crusty bread. The shells go clack clack like castanets.

Snake arms. The arms are held out to the side, shoulder level, then moved in undulations starting with the shoulder, the elbow and rippling down to the hands and fingers.

Wash the lettuce for the salad. One bowl for the children with just a little olive oil. Another for herself and Eamon with tomatoes, avocado, olives, fresh Parmesan and oil. Now just wait for the bread to warm. Check the clams. Steam puffed out giving off a nice smell. Table set for dinner. Clams brought in their pot, the two bowls of salad on either side, the breadbasket nearby. Back to the kitchen for two glasses of water and two glasses of wine. Call everyone to dinner.

Eamon had been home for a while but he was in the living room listening to music. He looked tired. She ruffled his hair and bent down to kiss him lightly on the lips.

"How were things at work?" she asked.

He looked up at her. "Not bad."

Margaret lifted the cover off the clams and went to get an extra bowl for the shells.

Shoulders back and forwards alternatively. Go faster and faster into a full shoulder shimmy. Slightly lean backwards alternatively. Then bring it forwards. Habibi.

Everyone had started eating by the time she got back to the dining room. The girls played with the clamshells.

"So, are you still on training?" Margaret asked her husband.

"Yeah."

"Will you have to wear a uniform?"

"Nah, it's not like that. I don't even have to leave the observation room. If I see something on the cameras, I call the police."

"Your study in film-making is probably a good thing so?"

"I wouldn't say that. I just watch the screen, store the DVDs and look for something if the police need it for an investigation. Not exactly Oscar material."

The children scurried off to play computer games. Eamon moved to the living room. He turned on the television and sat down to watch a match. Margaret cleared the table, turned on the coffee and put the dishes in the dishwasher. When the coffee was ready, she brought it in and sat down on the sofa beside her husband. She watched his profile as he sipped from his cup, eyes glued to the soccer match.

"When does the system start up?" she asked.

Eamon's chin jutted out but his head didn't turn away from the television.

"Monday week."

Margaret went upstairs. She took off her bulky sweater and tried the sticky belly-button jewel. Her tummy was too big but with the jewel, it looked round and feminine.

The camel. Arms either up or one crooked in front, the other cupping the bottom. Step and bring body until it can't go any further. Then cut and suck in the stomach. It should look like a slow sensuous wave.

The weather in the west of Ireland could change from one hour to the next. Indeed, it had been known to be different in the front of the house and the back at the same time. Rain could be streaming down the front window while sunbeams danced over their semi-wild garden out the back. After Easter the slightest bit of sunshine would bring people outdoors without a jacket, happy that for once it wasn't raining, yet worried that these few weak rays of sun would make up their entire summer.

And so Margaret found herself on a beach in Connemara in April, wading into cold water up to her thighs. Her two daughters were in long before. Margaret knew that their way was less painful in the long run but could not bring herself to make the plunge. Waves rolled and licked her sides in cool torture. Finally, she could stand it no longer and let the sea take her under. She shook the water from her hair as she surfaced and made several strokes farther out before turning back to join the girls. The water was bracing.

They joined hands to jump into the waves, the power knocking them down. The girls wrapped long strands of wide honey-coloured seaweed round their necks and performed a complicated dance routine in the water.

Margaret crouched down in the sea as she watched. The air was even colder than the water. Her hand disturbed something on the seabed. A crab wrapped its large front claw around her wrist but not in a threatening way. She brought her hand out of the water with the crab still hanging at her wrist like a bracelet. She gently disentangled herself from its grip. Clack Clack.

Hands. Hold in front, middle finger and thumb together but not touching and the other fingers out. Roll the hands at the wrist as if picking apples. Continue as you raise your arms above your head. Keep one arm above the head while dropping the other down framing the body. The hands become baby squid swimming through an ink-like ocean.

Margaret told the girls to put sweaters on when they got out. The wind had picked up, and the air turned cold when the sun went behind a cloud. On the drive home, bog land and stone-fenced fields passed in succession.

Her eye caught a beam of sunshine, strong and bright, before it faded. She held it in her mind. Sun. The warmth took her back to Morocco where she felt sun on bare skin. Dancing to the drumbeat, moving to the rhythm, not knowing what she doing but feeling the music in her bones.

It was there she first met Eamon. In the open, not closed in. Talking and touching into the black night. Where had all the dancing, talking and touching gone? In Ireland you could forget you had a body hiding under all the layers of clothes.

Finger cymbals are held on to the middle finger and thumb by elastic. Hit right-left-right. Faster. Right-left-right. Ratatatat.

Eamon's new job was the operator on the new CCTV cameras set up throughout the city. A special unit had come to train him. Most of the cameras were situated in potential trouble spots. Eamon had been in contact with an operator in Dublin where the system had been operating for almost a year now. He had been warned to expect close-ups of drunken vomiting and other unsavoury images. He was also told not to expect to do much about preventing crime. The cameras were only there to alert the Guards if a serious crime was taking place. He would have to go through old footage if the police needed it for a case. It wasn't going to be easy sitting there alone night after night.

His dreams would help to get him through it. "*Hot Shutter*, the crime fighter with the all-seeing camera. See him surprise the most wanted criminals and catch them red-handed in their dastardly deeds. Cleaning up Galway City. Hit film of the year!"

When Eamon actually started monitoring the cameras, it disrupted the whole family. He would have dinner and then go to work at seven in the evening until three in the morning. Everyone would have to tiptoe around the house in daytime so as not to wake him up. He began the job on a weekend and came home disgusted by the vomit, urination and fights caused by drink.

Margaret had borrowed a sewing machine and was making a top out of silk velvet she had hand-painted. The fabric was a light turquoise with tiny white Celtic designs etched in wax. The top was called a cholis. 'Indian', she thought. Just a bra with sleeves really.

Upstairs she had a long flowing skirt of turquoise silk and a shawl of fuchsia pink with coins along the edges. She put her sewing away as she heard Eamon stirring. He walked sleepily down the stairs, into the living room and sat down beside Margaret.

"What's it like, the monitoring room?" Margaret asked him.

"It's just a room with 30 television screens along one wall. It wouldn't be so bad if it wasn't so boring."

"What about the equipment?"

"It's first class, but one of the cameras has already been destroyed."

Margaret asked him where the cameras were. Eamon took out a diagram and went over where each one was, pointing out the broken one and how he saw a lad take a stick and bash it.

Then with Eamon off to work and with the children in bed, Margaret took a piece of paper and wrote camera one, camera two, right down to 30 in a column, one under each other.

Camera one – snake arms, showing only the left side

Camera two – torso shot doing chest circles

Camera three – snake arms, showing the right side

Camera four – shimmy (bottom shot)

When she was finished, she posted it up beside the mirror, changed into her costume and started the isolated moves. She practised until she was happy with the performance as a whole.

It was a daft idea. She didn't know why she was doing it. It would be better for her to just get on with her life and let Eamon adapt to his new job. But somehow she was compelled to go through with it. She set a date for the following Thursday night.

It was a spring evening – not raining but cloudy and cold.

"I can do it," she mouthed into the mirror.

She dressed in her costume when the children were in bed, greeted the babysitter, put on a long coat and walked into town. She had planned one move at each camera so it would form a collage of a whole dance. She had to be careful not to show her face.

Each move was so quick that she had very few hecklers. Just a drunk at a camera Eamon had pointed out as a problem one. She felt good when she finished.

Several days later Eamon watched her from bed as she was dressing, his head propped up lazily by his arm.

"I know it was you," he said.

Margaret said nothing but hesitated a second before pulling up her tights.

"We had a test a few nights ago. Sort of an opening. A launch of the camera programme. All the top brass was there. I know it was you Mags."

Margaret froze. Since there had been no mention of her dance, she had begun to think it had gone unnoticed and had been relieved.

"Yes, everyone congratulated me on what a great job I had. They all asked for copies of the night's video. All edited. You may as well inform me what music to mix with it." He sighed. "It's hard enough having to do the job with the poxy hours, the boredom, the drunks. Then to have my wife parading in front of everyone."

Margaret kept her eyes on the floor and opened her mouth to say something. She was going to say that she had wanted Eamon to dance with her so much that it hurt. Or at least to watch her dance. But she didn't.

The rain and wind had taught her well. She held her head high, smiled mysteriously at Eamon and walked out of the room.

WHAT DO YOU DO WITH A DRUNKEN POET?

"What about down the pier?" Aidan suggested to break the silence. He looked around the table at the other four who were looking for messages in their coffee.

"I mean, Terry loved that pier. He used to talk about all the coloured houses, the boats, the swans…"

"Yeah, right," interrupted Grainne, pouting her lovely lips and playing with the nib sticking out of her beret. "He liked to tell stories of cars going over the pier – watching people trapped – facing a slow watery death. Remember Li?"

Liam rattled the spoon around in his coffee cup. He looked at Grainne a long time without speaking. Everyone in the group knew that he and Grainne were an item but since they didn't seem to want it known, everyone pretended they didn't notice. Liam cleared his throat.

"Just because we're doing this thing doesn't mean we have to make Terry into all sweetness and light. Let's not forget that he was an ignorant fucker and a nasty drunk."

Imelda was the only person in the group over forty. She always spoke quietly. Some people were unkind, saying that she talked as if she were in outer space. She loved everyone.

"He was usually okay at our meetings here. He always

135

had good work and gave good criticism. A bit direct, perhaps. But spot on."

"That's because there was only coffee here," said Grainne. "It was another story at the bar."

"Look," said Aidan, "we're not here to dissect Terry's personality, complex as it was. We have to decide what to do with him. The sooner the better. We can't leave him like this."

"The sooner the better," echoed Imelda. "I have to get home to my kids."

Aidan looked at Paul, the youngest of the group, just out of secondary school and writing about dark things. "What do you think, Paul?"

Paul always tried to act older and deeper than he was. Pausing before he spoke as if he were an actor getting into a role, you could almost see a stringy beard as he stroked his bare chin. His voice came out lower than expected but with the familiar well-modulated tone. He could have made a great radio announcer.

"The Claddagh, might be an idea," he said to a chorus of sighs. "I mean, he was always there. He lived in the area. And it's the place ... well ... "

"That's because of that damn dog!" said Liam.

Grainne cut in. "He'd go down by the basin to give the dog a swim. He'd throw sticks in the water and watch the old mutt fetch them. Stupid dog! Half the time it would come back with a bunch of seaweed in its mouth. Then Terry would get it to chase swans into the water."

"Grainne's right. He used to tell me he went down there to see who had "jumped" over the weekend. He and that dog came across at least six bodies caught on the rocks there. Strange that now ... "

Everyone descended into silence once again and Paul volunteered to get more coffee. He went up to the counter and told the waiter that they were going to take longer than they thought. She smiled.

"That's always the way with you lot," she said. "No problem for regulars anyway. How long have you been meeting here anyway?" she asked, already knowing the answer but pretending to think hard.

"Well, I've been coming since January but the others have been coming forever."

"Forever's about five years then. Because that's how long the café's been open."

"But I think they met somewhere else before."

"Who knows?" The waitress said she was sorry about Terry. He had been a colourful addition to the place. She asked if they wanted the same again.

Paul nodded. When he arrived back at the table, Aidan was making another suggestion.

"What about a picnic? In a field. In Barna Woods?"

No one said anything.

"Well, on the street then. Say something. At least I have ideas!"

Their heads all snapped up like carrion birds eying dinner.

"This isn't like one of your precious poems," spat Liam.

He waved his index fingers in the air.

"This is not the search for universal beauty. It's Terry for godsakes! No one rawer than that."

"But gifted," added Grainne.

"Gifted," they all repeated.

"There's no denying that," mumbled Imelda.

Aidan nodded. "So what's wrong with a picnic in a field then? Say a few lines. Enjoy the day."

"He would have passed out in a field," said Liam.

"What fucking difference does that make? It's more for us than him. He wouldn't really give a dog's breakfast."

"We're getting nowhere," complained Imelda.

The waitress arrived with the coffee.

"Double expresso?" Grainne nodded.

"Café latte?" Liam put up his hand.

"Americano?" Aidan reached out to take it.

"Tea?" Imelda reached out to take it.

"Hot chocolate?" Paul cleared a place in front of him.

"And a large regular coffee?"

Silence. Then a general fidgeting. The waitress finally realized that the regular coffee was Terry's usual order. She placed the cup back on her tray, cleared away the dirty cups and started to walk away.

"The last ones are on the house," she whispered.

Unable to say anything, each member of the writers' group stared through the café's front window into the damp dark Galway street. Aidan fingered the small box in his jacket pocket.

Breaking the stillness, he got up and went to the men's toilet. He took out the carved stone box he had bought on his travels to Afghanistan. Taking a deep breath, he opened it, poured the contents down the toilet and flushed.

Aidan watched as the others finished their drinks and talked on. They hadn't noticed his silence. After a while, they seemed to come to some agreement and Liam turned to Aidan.

"Where are they?" he asked.

"What?"

"The ashes. Terry's ashes."

Aidan put up his hands in resignation.

"I've already done it lads! he said. "I've flushed Terry down the friggin' toilet."

And suddenly he didn't care what they thought. Terry had loved this café and here he'd stay. Not literally. But in a way.

"Yeah, write a poem about that one lads," he chuckled.

GIVE THE DOG A TUNE

I was responsible for ruining the life of my best friend. Well, temporarily at least. Collin Joyce and I had been meeting down at Seamus Connolly's pub every Thursday night for twenty years. We'd watch the match, have a few pints and the craic. There was chat too, great goals, the latest scandal on the news, films we'd seen and books we'd read.

Collin appeared to enjoy life. He was good company and could recite a poem at the drop of the hat without boring everyone stiff. I had no doubt he was a great teacher. His wife Phyllis and their five children surrounded him with a joyful swarm of activity.

His one passion besides his family was his dog, a black and white border collie, Muddle. Whenever Collin called, the dog would come bounding and off they would go, exploring along the canal, through the university with all its trees or perhaps over to the lake for a quick swim before the swans got possessive and started closing in. At night the dog lay protectively by his side as he sat reading by the fire. Collin would have allowed Muddle to curl at the end of the bed but his wife refused.

"You never know where they've been," she said.

Muddle took his place in his own bed under the stairs

while Collin pressed himself against the warmth of his wife's body.

Thursday nights weren't the only nights I met up with Collin. There were poker games, special matches, the odd concert, Christmas get-togethers. I always looked forward to the Thursday nights though. I would lock up my shop and spend a moment gazing at the wooden sign hanging outside: "Joe Tynan, Musical Instruments." Then I would go to Mc Donagh's for fish and chips and, if it weren't too busy, linger over a newspaper until it was time to meet Collin at Seamus's. If the restaurant was crowded, I'd walk down by the Claddagh or through town to look in shop windows, something I couldn't do during the day when I was working. By the time I strolled into the pub, Collin was usually there before me, sitting back with a pint in front of him and another ordered for me.

It was just before his 45th birthday. I came in expecting a pint on the table.

"I thought we'd have a whiskey," he said. "Just for a change."

"What are we celebrating?"

"Not a fucking thing!" he said in language that was not characteristic of him.

With that he raised his glass in a toast, drank and for a while he was silent. He glanced over at me.

"You're lucky. You were in that rock band."

"That was more than twenty years ago."

"What was the name? Don't tell me ... The Slime?"

"No, actually it was *The Ooze.*"

"That's it. It was great."

"We were young."

"But you still play."

"It's not exactly *The Ooze*. A couple of us oldies play jazz on weekends at Simmon's Hotel."

"But still ... "

We were always comfortable with our own thoughts. Silence was never a problem between us. We attended to the whiskey and watched the barman Seamus put pints roughly down on the bar. To those who did not know him, he appeared gruff and unpleasant. It was a pub for locals.

"Are you sticking to the whiskey?" I asked as I got up. It was my round. Collin just held up his empty glass. I went back on the porter. "I believed the ads. Guinness is good for you."

"What brought that up?"

"What up?"

"The thing about the band, about *The Ooze* ... "

He took a sip of whiskey.

"I was just wondering how you were able to join a band and all."

"I was there man, that's all."

"You know, Joe. I'll be forty-five next week."

"I know."

"And I've done nothing with my life. I've always wanted to learn a musical instrument."

I didn't know what to say. So I kept quiet.

"I used to laugh at all those middle-aged men and their unfulfilled dreams. And here I am right there in the same stupid place."

"You have your job ... " I started.

"Don't lecture me." He held up his hand, palm out. "I have Phil telling me that I can finish everything in my next life. Suppose I'll be plucking a sitar. Or that strange instrument played on Shop Street by the fat guy wearing the kilt and the hat with the feather. What if I came back as a dung beetle? What would I play then?"

Losing patience with him, I lashed out. "If you want to learn something, just do it."

"But what would I learn?"

"What do you mean?"

"What instrument? You're the expert."

I didn't know what he wanted from me. But I hated seeing him like this. He had always been so content. On impulse I wanted to give him what he thought he lacked; a musical voice, a way to express himself, to reproduce notes into meaning.

While he was getting the last round, I thought of a plan.

* * *

The party was not a surprise. It would have been difficult to keep it from him since it was held at his house and preparations had to be made. There was just a small group of friends for dinner with lots of wine. The children joined us for a meal and then drifted off. Phil placed a pile of gifts in front of Collin.

"Don't keep us in suspense any longer. Open them." she said.

Some people took their time opening gifts, gently peeling off each piece of sellotape so as not to tear the paper.

Collin was more of a ripper. Heaps of paper fell tumbling around him. Earlier in the day he had received gifts from his offspring: socks, more socks, cologne he would never wear, a miniature chess set. Now from his friends, a DVD, a book of short stories, a bottle of whiskey. And from Phil, a case of wine.

"Something we can share," she said.

Mine came in a big box. It was amusing to watch him open it.

"There's nothing in here," he said.

Then he noticed the business card at the bottom of the box.

"What are you doing Tynan? Getting a little publicity in?"

Not letting on that I remembered what he had revealed a few days previously, I said:

"A man should play some type of instrument in his life. I'm going to lend you one instrument every month until you find one suited to you. I also have a list of reasonably-priced instructors. We'll have you playing in a band yet."

Collin went for the big ones first. A few days after his birthday I helped him load a keyboard into his car. He set it up in the spare room and practiced with a teacher once a week.

After a month I asked him if he wanted to stick to it.

"Perhaps," he said. "I'd like to try something else first, though."

"Try a button accordion. It's related but different."

It too was returned at the end of the next month. I

did not mean the uileann pipes when I suggested he try something more in the Irish traditional scene. After the first week, he was relegated to the back shed. Muddle howled along with the pipes, the children shouted in protest and Phil threatened to leave him. He looked slightly paler and scruffier when he brought them back.

"Perhaps not the pipes," he said. "You have to be born to them."

As he went on to string instruments, Muddle had acquired an accomplished accompanying voice. Sometimes other dogs on the street joined in too.

On the eighth month, Collin's wife Phil phoned me at the shop.

"I can't stand it, Joe. I know you meant well but it's torture. Besides the noise, he spends all his time at it, has no time to do things around the house, no time for the kids. I haven't had a real conversation with him for months and am worried we will get out of practice."

"Calm down Phil," I said.

"Because if he doesn't stop, I'm going to have to ask him to leave, him and that dog."

"I'll give him something gentler this time."

I thought he couldn't do much harm with a recorder. He had had it for about two weeks when he came into the shop.

"How are you getting on?" I asked.

"Oh, great."

I carried on stacking shelves as he shuffled back and forth on his feet. I wondered if he perhaps needed to go to the toilet.

"I see you have a gig this Saturday."

"Yeah, nine o'clock."

He sometimes went along and I would join him during the breaks. Phil even dropped in occasionally.

"I couldn't join you this once?" he asked.

"Sure, you often do."

"No," he said. "Not like that. As part of the band."

I didn't see what harm he could do. When he showed up on the night, I consulted the other members of the band, telling them that Collin wouldn't be availing of the mic.

"Are you sure about this?" I asked Collin.

"Absolutely. I've been going great guns on the flute … er, recorder."

It was a nice crowd and after finishing the set, we stopped for a beer. Collin seemed elated and a bit hyper. The beer made him bolder during the next set and he moved in closer to the microphone. I could hear the false notes and cringed. He knew only one song, 'Au Claire de la Lune' or something like that, which he tried to adapt to the rest of the music of the band. He didn't even play that song well.

At the next break, the manager took me aside.

"What's with your man?"

"Just jammin' with us."

"Well, lose him. He stinks."

The lads were quiet, looking into their pints as Collin sipped his beer and tried to make conversation. I put my pint on the table and sat down beside him.

"Listen Collin the manager is just after telling me that no one without a union card can play in his bar. Sorry mate."

The others were trying to hide their relief. I could see

them trying to work out the thing about union cards. That was something I'd picked up from TV. I could tell that Collin was disappointed. He had enjoyed being part of the band, strutting his stuff upon the stage.

"That's alright man. I've had a taste of it."

"It's not *Ooze* you know, Collin. It's *Sometimes Vertical.* Big difference."

"Yeah, I know. But it was cool."

As much as Collin seemed to enjoy the recorder, it came back to the shop in return for a tin whistle.

"For the love of God, Joe," Phil pleaded on the phone one day. "This has got to stop. Those shrill notes have me demented. Even the dog is hiding under the table."

"We haven't even got around to percussion," I joked.

"I'm warning you Joe."

"Ok, I'll find something else. There's not much time left anyway."

The next month he went home with wooden spoons joined together at the top. He cracked them all over his body as he had seen an old man do.

"Dance Muddle. Dance. Good boy."

Unfortunately, once he hit them together just a little too hard and the wood split in two.

"I'm so sorry Joe. Tell me how much they are and I'll pay you."

"Don't worry about it."

"I was getting on great with them."

"Well, it's the last month. I'll give you something like the spoons but more durable."

I pulled out two sticks that looked like ivory.

"What's that?" asked Collin.

"The bones," I replied. "The bones."

Collin didn't find them as easy as the spoons because they weren't joined at the top but he kept at it. The noise wasn't excessive and Phil had settled down. Birthday 46 was around the corner.

I'll bring the bones back tomorrow," Collin told me on the phone. "Then we'll talk."

However, when Collin went downstairs the next morning, he couldn't see them.

"Phil, have you put them anywhere?" he asked.

"No," Phil answered, even though Collin knew that she had no idea what he was asking about.

"It's ok. I'll look later. I'll just take the dog for a walk first."

When Muddle heard the word 'walk' he sprang to the door from his bed under the stairs and waited for the lead to be put on.

"There you go Muddle. C'mon boy."

Suddenly realising something, Collin took a closer look at his dog, watching the little pink tongue slide over his thin black lips. Examining the bed under the stairs, he found white slivers. Muddle looked up at him with a hangdog expression.

"It's okay boy. A fitting end to my music career!" Collin laughed.

Man and dog, Collin with a poem in his head, scampered along the street to a large field behind the boys' school where Muddle fetched, then chewed up the sticks Collin threw for him.

When I phoned to wish Collin a happy birthday, Phil said he was out with the dog.

"And Joe," she said. "We're just having a small family dinner this year."

GETTING LOST

"I think you should talk to this one," the secretary said rolling her eyes.

There were courses a few times a year at our language school to train people to teach English to foreigners in Ireland or abroad. We were taking registrations for the next course, a job in which I usually didn't get involved as the secretary was efficient in dealing with queries. However, this one day a woman burst into my office and looked down at me with black smouldering eyes. Johnny Depp I thought, Johnny Depp eyes. The secretary was ready to tell her to wait outside but I said it was okay and told the woman to sit down.

"I'm Declan O'Byrne," I said. "What seems to be the problem?"

She looked at me with dismissal, blowing out a quick burst of air from between pursed lips.

"The Problem? Well, Declan, the problem is that I want to go on the TEFL course."

She was seething. Her accent was right out of all those New York series on television when I was growing up. I found her enchanting.

"And that's a problem?" I queried.

She calmed down, cocked her head to the side looking at me directly in the eyes and shrugged. I thought I could make out the faintest traces of a smile.

"I have the money. A friend is going to lend it to me. The problem is that I've done lots of things but I've never finished college."

"Oh," I said. One of the requirements for the course was a third level degree.

She persisted, telling me that she had gone to a junior college, had taught English before and had had plenty of experience with foreigners. It was as though she were flirting with me, rolling her black eyes demurely. I tried to concentrate, to think of a solution but was distracted by her intensity.

"Experience eh?" I echoed.

"Yeah, experience."

I told her that in some cases a candidate could be accepted on terms of life experience instead of a university degree.

The girl perked up, someone accustomed to always finding a loophole.

"Don't get too excited!" I explained that those who entered the course under such circumstances would only be able to work abroad and had to sign a document that they wouldn't seek teaching work inside the Republic of Ireland.

"No problem. Planning on going away anyway. Somewhere sunny."

Something felt a bit wrong but I shrugged it off and shoved an application form across the desk telling her to complete it, and to add a paragraph about how her life experience would help in her teaching. I wanted to make her happy. Often a lost soul myself, I believed everyone should be given a chance.

In a few days the form was back on my desk: Tracy Brummel, Age 27, Born: New York. My mind formed the picture of her whole body moving like a shrug that told the world she didn't give a damn. I could see her black eyes floating in front of me staring, saying 'don't you dare refuse me'.

The writing was excellent. Reading through the reasons why her experience would help her teaching, the streets of New York came back to me: the throngs of feet on the avenues, the sophisticated mannequins in shop windows, the energy coming from so many busy minds together. Noise jolted me out of complacency. The mixture of cultures dazzled me. The arts cried out at me. New York City seeped into me.

I was stranded in New York at 19 on my way back from Latin America. I was supposed to stay with a distant cousin, John Phillip Sousa III, who was an editor with Fortune Magazine and related through the Adams and the Flanigans. I had run out of money and couldn't fly home. My mother had wired him enough for me to buy a ticket. And I had expected to stay with this Sousa although I had never met him. It was a practice common where I was from. Family was family!

My oversized suitcase stood close against a table in a Cuban restaurant in Manhattan where my cousin lived.

(To me knapsacks were only for serious mountaineers and continentals.) I had enough money for a meal and some wine and kept phoning my cousin, but he was never there. After a few hours I met a young couple and, as I still hadn't got in touch with my cousin, they invited me home to their Central Park Apartment.

With the confidence of youth that everything would work out eventually, I went with them to their huge living space. I can't remember their names but he was Jewish and worked in films or television. She was Chinese and a concert pianist, her black grand piano stark against white marble floors. We shared another bottle of wine.

My cousin was at home when I phoned the next morning. He was not very nice. Slightly friendlier in his apartment, he said: "I thought you were going to be some goddamn hippy." He gave me the money my mother had sent me to buy a ticket home to Dublin. Later taking some time to have a drink with him, I found out that he was actually rather nice. Then I was on my way. Waltzing through New York. Not a bother on me.

I suppose I was still thinking of the energy of New York when I picked up the phone and asked Tracy to come in to sign the release form and pay the deposit. She was down within the hour.

"It's not that big a thing," I said as she hugged me and passed me the form.

"Yeah. It is," she said. "Thanks."

What I didn't know was that her friends were really pushing for the course. There was a whole group of supportive

Irish women saying, "If only you do the course…" or "Just do the course and you'll be grand."

The course was demanding but enjoyable, three full weeks of intensive training: learning to teach in an interesting way, dealing with grammar, listening, reading and writing.

In one peer practise, a girl asked Tracy why she had come to Ireland. For a moment Tracy just stood there looking stricken like an animal caught in headlights, black eyes darting from side to side, looking for a way out. Then she started moving her arms and then her legs, getting into her 'attitude' stance, her head tilted back.

"I wanted to lose someone," she said.

Most times she was funny. Everyone wanted to be around her; I wanted to be around her. In these courses participants get fairly close. They confide in one another and encourage each other. Everyone loved Tracy.

When the theory part of the course had finished, it was time to go on to actual teaching. I paired Tracy with a quiet teacher trainee called Siobhan thinking they would be effective together. It seemed to work. Tracy's outgoing and comic personality took Siobhan's mind off herself, and Siobhan's gentleness and caring gave Tracy the attention she needed.

When dealing with real students, Tracy and Siobhan were given a beginners class made up of Spanish, Japanese and Italians. The subject was 'the weather in the past'.

'What was it like out yesterday?' Siobhan wrote on the board and then went through many possible variations of weather. The students listened and repeated. Photocopies were handed out and the students took turns reading out the dialogues.

"What was it like out yesterday?"

"It was sunny."

They read the various responses. Then without the paper, they would improvise answers with flash cards.

"What was the weather like?"

"It was foggy."

Siobhan praised them when they got it right. Then Tracy took over with freer practice. Students picked out paper squares with a picture on it as a cue for dialogue and then improvised. Tracy jumped up and down after each correct dialogue surprising the students.

"All right!" she said in her expressive New York accent.

"All right!" copied the students in unison.

Soon they were shouting back everything she said. It came out as a wild chant.

"Kentaro and Pilar, you try. What was ... ?"

"What was the weather like yesterday?" a Japanese boy asked a Spanish girl.

"It was raining," she answered.

An Italian boy who was slightly more advanced became adventurous.

"Are you sure?" he asked.

"Yes," replied Pilar. "Going to school, I wet myself`."

I was watching Tracy to see what she would do. It would play right into her sense of humour but laughter could shake the confidence needed in the first baby steps of learning a language. I could see Siobhan stifling a

155

giggle. The other students didn't seem to have noticed.

Tracy looked at the girl and then turned to the board.

"Very good, Pilar. But we usually say it like this." She repeated what she wrote on the board. "I got wet."

Pilar repeated the phrase followed by the whole class. They all sounded very New Yorkish.

It was then that I decided that Tracy would make a good teacher. I told her so during the break over coffee.

"The people stuff is ok," she said. "Even the project. It's the exam I'm worried about."

She went on to say that she always froze writing exams.

"I guess that's why I never finished college."

I assured her that she would be fine, that there was nothing on the test that wasn't covered during the course.

It was held on the Saturday after classes finished. Tracy arrived looking nervous.

"You have three hours," I said. "Take your time and read the questions carefully."

The trainee teachers started scanning down the paper and then started to write. I stood at the top of the room and busied myself with a book. Three-quarters of an hour into the exam, Tracy got out of her seat, walked up to my desk and threw the exam paper down.

"I can't do this," she said.

"Tracy, you know all of it. Just try. You can do it."

"That's what people keep telling me. But I can't," she wheezed, rushing past me and slamming the door. Later I tried to phone her to say that she could re-sit the exam at any time. No answer.

The other students asked about Tracy but no one had heard from her. Everyone else passed. When the diplomas arrived from the Department of Education, I met the trainee teachers for a drink at one of the pubs along the canal.

It was hot but the back door onto the canal was shut. When Siobhan asked if we could open it, the barman told us the door had been blocked off by the police. A Spanish tourist had discovered a body floating in the canal the night before.

"Oh, my God," said Siobhan, "what is it with these teenage boys that they want to destroy themselves?"

"It wasn't a boy," said the barman. We were silent so he continued. "It was a woman. An American, police told me."

We looked from one to another. The barman had nothing more to tell us despite our desperate questions for more information.

When the newspaper came out the following Thursday, Tracy's face stared out at me from the front page. I found myself wishing life into those night-black eyes, to sense again the bit of toughness that sliced through Irish civility. At the same time, I wanted to close those same eyes gently and tell her that the pain was gone.

Shaking my head at the thought that her death was in some way my fault, I dismissed the idea that it had been the test that had pushed her over the edge.

'I came here to lose someone' echoed in my ears, and I realized that 'the someone' Tracy wanted to lose was herself.

FOR A SONG

The doorbell broke the calm of a sunny spring day in a leafy neighbourhood in Dublin's southside. Being the only one in the house, Brooke closed her books and ran down the stairs to answer the door. She recognised the man standing there, his finger in mid air, ready to press the button one more time.

"Grocery delivery for Miss Louise Talbot," he smiled.

"Hello, Lorcan," Brooke said as she took the plastic bag from him.

"I thought you had to spend a minimum amount to have things delivered. And it's basically just around the corner."

"That's ok. Miss Talbot is a regular customer and we had to drive this way anyway."

"It's nice of you, Lorcan."

"Well, ever since her accident, we've always looked out for her. Her losing strength in her arm. Not being able to carry things."

Brooke stood there with a confused look on her face.

"What?" She was going to say 'what accident?' but cut herself short. The actions of Weasie Talbot were not hers to question. Probably just another one of her schemes that allowed her to survive on next to nothing.

"Are you staying around much longer?"

"I have my exams at Trinity in a few weeks. I'll stick around for the summer, do some riding."

"Oh, you ride?"

"That's why I'm here. Irish horses and all that. They're great."

"So we get to keep you a little while longer," he said. "Well, I'd best be going. Some people get worked up if I'm late with their groceries. I'll see you around."

Brooke nodded and watched him walk down the driveway to his van. He looked good in jeans.

Blushing when he turned around before getting in the van, she gave a little wave. She thought he had flirted with her. There was an extra twinkle in his blue eyes as they slowly looked up under long dark lashes. Perhaps he was just being friendly. The Irish and their charm! Anyway, her books were to be her only company for the next while. She had to do well. It was costing her parents a fortune.

Brooke had just settled at her desk when her mind drifted out to the voluminous chestnut tree outside her window. Birds hopped from branch to branch singing into the spring air. It was difficult to concentrate. With great effort she managed to begin to focus on her studies when the phone rang.

"Hello," she answered after running downstairs to the hall.

"Ah, good girl, Brooke, You're there. Lorcan may come by with the groceries."

Weasie was shouting excitedly as always into the phone.

"He's already been."

"That's great, dear. I didn't want to carry the bag into town."

Brooke's dad had said that distant relatives should remain just that – distant. However, when Brooke was accepted at Trinity and at Lauren Kelles' Riding School, her mother had immediately thought of her Irish second cousin once removed.

"Louise – Weasie we had always called her- is a real character. You'll love her."

"I thought you said she was a fruitcake," her father interrupted.

"Well, she's a bit eccentric. That's because she's an arty type. She's an actress."

"You told me she lived with a god-damned bunch of cats."

"Yes, she did last time I checked. But she lives in a nice old house in a good safe area."

"There are lots of nice areas of Dublin. The Ambassador lives in one of them. Killiney. Nice place."

"The Ambassador is hardly going to take in our daughter as a lodger. Anyway, we don't even know him. I would feel better that she was with someone we knew. I'm sure Weasie could do with the money."

Brooke wandered out of the room half way through her father's next argument but could still hear.

"And you last saw this cousin, when? About thirty years ago?"

But her mother always won. Her father would give in after putting up a good fight.

So while her mother was making the arrangements for her stay in Dublin, Brooke had nightmares of staying in a spooky old house on a hill, cats crawling all over her and a mad woman lurking in the shadows.

It wasn't like that at all. The house, pleasant if not a bit run-down, stood on a bright cheerful street. Weasie did collect strays but they remained in the garden. The inside of the house was clean and decorated in artistic chic which disguised the shabbiness. Weasie – or Aunt Weasie as she called her – was far from a gaunt vampire type creeping around the corners. She was exotic, flamboyant and, as her profession demanded, dramatic.

After letting Brooke settle in for a few days, Weasie called her down to the parlour one night.

"What's say we make a dent in that excellent bottle of duty-free Tanqueray you brought me?"

"I don't really drink gin," she ventured. Brooke was astonished. She had never had a drink with her parents or any other old person before. Her mother had told her about the last time she visited Weasie. Laughing, she had said: "You just have to bring her a bottle. She likes gin. Tanqueray. Gordon's if they don't have it."

Weasie held up the bottle and Brooke couldn't help noticing that there was a fair amount gone already.

"Everyone likes gin. Here we go. Ice. Nice wedge of lemon. Tonic."

Brooke had no option but to take the glass. They toasted.

"To your stay with us."

She looked around vaguely to see who else made up the 'us' Weasie had mentioned and took a sip of the drink.

"Not bad."

Much later when the bottle was almost finished, Brooke got the courage to ask Weasie about her personal life.

"How come you never married?" she asked.

"Married."

"Yes, why didn't you?"

"He was married. I was the bit on the side. Fiddled my life away with him and then I was too old."

She poured herself another glass. The tonic and ice had run out.

"Not wasted, exactly. It was glorious. And he's still my best friend."

The crystal glasses rattled a bit when she started to dance. Then she burst into song. Grabbing Brooke to her feet, she said:

"I was once the belle of the ball. I could sing. I could dance. I could act."

"My mother still sings some of the songs you taught her. That one 'Foggy Dew', she especially liked."

"Well, let's sing it then."

If the gin didn't actually bind them together, singing did. Weasie discovered that Brooke had a reasonable voice. They spent many more nights singing into the early morning –sometimes songs from Weasie's musicals, sometimes songs Brooke knew. Weasie would break it up by reciting a poem or a monologue from one of the plays she had acted in. Brooke's letters home were full of enthusiasm for her life with Weasie.

It had been awhile since the last delivery of groceries. Brooke was starting to panic. Exams at Trinity seemed like such a big deal. She was memorizing birth dates of famous Irish poets when the doorbell rang.

"Can you get that dear? I'm in the bath."

Annoyed that her studies were interrupted, Brooke opened the door to find Lorcan.

"I have Ms. Talbot's delivery here."

"But she hasn't been out today. She's still in the bath."

"She may be there now. But she was in the shop just after opening time. Had the whole place in stitches, copying the new security guard. How serious he is! You know what she's like when she gets going."

Lorcan handed over the small bag that Brooke held up to the light.

"You are being abused, Lorcan," she laughed. "No way there's twenty euro's worth in there."

"It's worth it just to see her slag off that bastard of a guard."

Brooke studied uninterrupted into the evening until Weasie came bursting into her room.

"We are going to eat tonight," she said. "Foster McKaye is having a launch. There will be the best of food and drink."

Brooke rubbed her eyes.

"You go along," she said. "I'll just help myself to a sandwich or order a pizza. I'm running out of studying time. Too many launches during term." She winked at Weasie who winked back and curtsied low.

"How do I look?"

In fiery red to match her hair, she was spectacular.

"You don't know what you're missing!" she called back as she left the room.

Living hand to mouth as a poor actress for years, Weasie had been teaching Brooke how to survive. She brought her to every book and art launch, telling her outright that there would be no dinner for her at home so that she should eat and drink as much as possible. Weasie had also developed an interest in Brooke's riding practice, turning up to watch and cheer her on. She ended up becoming a sort of an eccentric pet of the horsey set and dined out on her connection with Brooke.

The weather was getting better and better, and by the time Brooke was sitting her exams, it was sweltering.

"This is our summer," said Weasie. "Go out for a walk or you will miss it."

Eventually, the last exam was completed. Since Brooke didn't know many of the other students well enough to go celebrating with them, she went home. Weasie was always one to celebrate.

"Your first year at Trinity finished." She almost looked sentimental. "Come on. We've been invited to a party with some actor friends of mine in Howth, the other side of Dublin Bay. You'll have to have your party piece ready. There will be singing. Someone will say a poem. There will be music."

Weasie picked up her woven red and orange handbag and extracted a small orange purse. There were only a few coins inside.

"What have you got?"

"Me? Nothing 'til the end of the month when my grant comes in."

Weasie twisted Brooke's hair and tied it back with a raven decorated comb.

"I have an idea," she said. "Follow me."

She led Brooke around the corner to the supermarket. All the staff seemed to know her well. With her basket in hand, she started to select various items and then, appearing satisfied, she went to the sales counter.

"That's €20, Weasie," the sales clerk said.

Weasie handed over her visa card.

"I'll have that delivered, pet."

"Just fill out the card for me then."

She wrote:

Name: Louise Talbot

Address: 99A The Howth Road

Dublin

Then walking out into the car park, she spotted the white van. Groceries were being rolled out and loaded while Lorcan sat patiently behind the wheel.

"Hello, Lorcan," she said.

Weasie waited until Lorcan was alone. He was clutching a list of addresses in his hand.

"I noticed that one of your deliveries was to Howth. We just happen to be going there too. So we may as well hop in with you."

The Howth run was the longest on Lorcan's list, the others located within a short distance of the supermarket.

When they arrived at the house, Weasie thanked Lorcan and whispered:

"Now won't you take that bag of groceries and leave it at the side of the house under the rosemary bush?"

Lorcan knew he'd been had, but because Weasie was as she was, he didn't mind much. In fact, he returned later that night with other members of the trad band he was in.

Lorcan and Brooke got a lot closer that night and are still together. I could tell you how they got home again that night but that would be another story.

- fin -